From the Rise Universe

by

Mandy Collins-Moore

CM Stars Publications from CM Stars Creations
https://www.cmstarscreations.com/cm-stars-publications

Published 2023.

Contents

Dear Reader,

The release of the first story in the *Sandbox* corner of The Rise Universe has been far too long in coming. I started it right after *Rise Mind Over Matter* was released, but a great many things hindered the process. There were life & health issues I did not see coming, and while those things did slow the progression of *Sandbox* down, I don't feel they were the main cause of the delays. The biggest cause of the delays was me. I'd get several pages or even chapters written and find they just didn't feel right, they didn't speak to me. Knowing if they didn't speak to me, they wouldn't speak to you, I'd scrap them and begin fresh. There were a few times I decided I was simply overthinking it and went forward with announcing release dates, each time something delayed it. At least one of those times, I believe some sort of intervention took place because my software went completely nuts and corrupted the file. I was furious and frustrated at the time, but looking back on it, I'm glad it happened because that version of *Sandbox* was not what it should have been.

I feel the story and characters were leading me to where I was meant to go with this story. I have always believed a writer should listen to their characters and trust them. I had failed to do that with *Sandbox* in the beginning, and boy, did they teach me a lesson for that. Once I stopped fighting them, they took me on a wonderful if sometimes heartbreaking adventure, and I hope they do the same for you. I sincerely hope I have done their journey justice, as well as lived up to your expectations.

As you read this, I am working on the next addition to The Rise Universe, *City of Hope*, along with the third installment of *Rise*. Soon, you will also see the release of a new series I am working on, Hearts and Stars. This series will be considerably different than what most of you have come to expect from me, but it is something I have wanted to do for a long time, and I am particularly passionate about it. The first two releases from the series will be *Like the Waltons* and *Popaw's Country*

Store. I hope you will join me on those journeys as well. To keep up with progress and release dates for *City of Hope*, the third *Rise* installment, *Like the Waltons*, or *Popaw's Country Store* keep an eye on our website, cmstarscreations.com, or join our Discord, CM Stars Creations Town Square. You can find a link to join the Discord via my Twitter, @MandyC_Moore. I'd love to see you there!

Thank you so much for the support you have shown for my work, and I hope I continue to earn that support. Now, welcome to *Sandbox*!

Much Love and Hugs!
Mandy

P.S. Don't forget, keep reaching for the stars!

ACKNOWLEDGEMENTS

A big thank you to Capp00, GrayGhostZoro, Hobo-Jesus, and J.C.'s Channel for agreeing to be part of this and helping to grow The Rise Universe. You are all truly impressive humans and excellent examples of the wonderful people in the gaming community and the world in general.

Thank you to all who welcomed me into the community and showed love and support for this series. There are entirely too many of you amazing folks to list, but you are each greatly appreciated. You will always have a special place in my heart.

JC, I cannot thank you enough for entrusting me with two of your most iconic characters. You will never know what an honor and a privilege it has been for me. I can only hope I have made you proud and used one of them to pay proper homage to Mr. Romero, someone we both adored.

Michael, thank you for believing in all my crazy ideas and schemes, even when some of them failed. I love you!

Special thanks to Lori Miller for saving me from the hell that is typing and not releasing any spoilers. You have been a lifesaver!

JC watched the Virginia countryside roll by as Mike steered the SUV along the bumpy, winding dirt road. While JC couldn't deny the beauty of the area, he couldn't figure out what Mike found so important he'd had him fly in from Chile.

"Cousin, you know I love you like a brother, but I am beginning to think you've lost your marbles," JC told Mike. "Where are we going, man?"

Mike glanced over with a grin. "Relax. I promise you're going to love it."

"Love what?"

Mike pointed ahead of them. "That."

Initially thinking a glare on the windshield was causing him to see things in a distorted manor, JC leaned up to get a better look. It took a moment for him to realize he was in fact seeing what appeared to be the top of a castle peeking out from above the trees. "What the hell?"

Mike beamed with pride. "Magnificent, isn't it?"

Soon Mike brought the SUV to a stop in front of a medieval village, complete with a castle. The grounds were horribly overgrown, and the buildings were quite rundown. Nevertheless, it was still a medieval village hidden away in the hills of Virginia.

"Explain," JC demanded.

As they explored the village, Mike told JC the story behind Virginia's unlikely medieval town and how he'd come to find it. Mike had been in Virginia for work when there'd been a delay on one of the projects he was heading up. He could have gone back home to Texas until things were resolved, but he'd decided to use the down time as a mini vacation and get to know more of Virginia. He'd rented the SUV and started visiting sites and areas the locals told him about. On one of those outings he had gotten lost in an area with unreliable cell reception. He was initially very frustrated, but then he stumbled across the village. His frustration quickly gave way to curiosity and wonder. He spent some time exploring it before forcing himself to leave and find his way back to civilization and the bed and breakfast he was staying in. After grabbing a bite to eat, he'd went back to his room and pulled out his laptop. He wanted to find out everything he could about the village, including who owned it.

Through his research he learned it had once been a Renaissance faire. The faire had been extremely popular at one time with visitors coming from across the country to experience it firsthand. It was so successful during its first few years of operation the company had made plans to expand it, but those plans would never see fruition. Business began to decline, visitors citing the heat and insects as the main reasons they stopped going. The company struggled to keep the faire open for a few more years but ultimately closed it for good in the late nineties. The village had been left to rot ever since.

JC smacked a mosquito that had landed on his arm. "It is a tad warm for fall, and the mosquitoes are the size of pelicans."

"Look past that," Mike pled. "Picture the grounds cleaned up and landscaped. Picture the buildings completely restored and new buildings of the same style or complimentary styles intermingled with them."

"Why should I do that?"

Mike nervously took a deep breath before launching into an impassioned explanation. He wanted to buy the village, restore it, build new additions, and turn it into a community for creative and intelligent people, the "nerds" of the world. It would be a place where they could live and work together with complete freedom from the unkind judgements and taunts so many still heaped upon them. In this community "nerdy" kids would be revered instead of tormented. "Geeky" adults would be surrounded by like-minded people. They would gladly accept and welcome those who also accepted them.

"Sounds like a hippie commune," JC teased.

"Seriously?!"

JC sighed. "Seriously, I love the idea. A whole town where creativity and intelligence are nurtured and celebrated would be amazing on every level, but you must be realistic. This is a massive undertaking, and the cost will be astronomical."

Mike rolled his eyes. "Come on! We've both made more money than we'll ever need in our lives. As for the heat and bugs, if we can't figure out a solution, we know enough scientists and engineers that one of them will be able to come up with something. With the right materials and contractors salvaging these buildings and constructing new ones it will be a breeze. In short, it's all simply a case of mind over matter."

"So, you want me to invest in this?"

“I want you to be my partner, my co-founder,” Mike beamed. “I want this to be the eutopia we both retire to and live out our golden years with people we can relate to.”

“Under one condition. I can make the appropriate fortifications.”

Mike rolled his eyes again.

“Mock me if you wish,” JC retorted, “but there is no doubt in my mind this world is heading for a catastrophic event. If it turns out I am wrong, which it will not, then no harm, no foul.”

“Can you do it without making the place look like an army bunker?”

“Um, yes. Yes, I believe I can do that.”

A big smile spread across Mike’s face as he held his hand out to JC to shake. “Alright then, partner.”

Three months later, after negotiating an acceptable purchase price, Mike and JC closed on their very own medieval village and wasted no time getting to work. Their first order of business was to hire a crew to help them clear the property of debris and overgrowth, a task that took several weeks. They then had each structure on the property evaluated to determine which ones were salvageable. To their delight, only two were deemed to be completely beyond salvation, and the castle was among the salvageable. They decided to use materials from the two buildings that couldn’t be salvaged to build unique structures and features in the courtyard they planned to build behind the castle.

From there they had the first of three of the new

buildings resurrected, two houses and a workshop. The workshop was very large to accommodate many of the materials and tools they anticipated needing in the restoration of existing structures as well as the construction of new structures and features. One of the two houses was for Mike and the other was for JC. Each house was specifically designed to suit the personality and style of its new owner.

Mike's house very much reflected the medieval theme of the town but did incorporate some basic modern comforts such as electricity, running water, appliances, and televisions, but that was the extent of how much he would allow the modern world to creep into his new home. His reasoning behind it was he spent all day every day working with some of the most advanced technology in the world and wanted his home to reflect a simpler life. In stark contrast, JC considered technology to be life, despite the fact he'd grown quite fond of the medieval architecture since they'd bought the village. As a result, his home was equipped with every modern convenience found in most homes along with some that only a tech obsessed scientist would install in a home. JC did take measures to ensure it was all cleverly designed to blend in with the medieval style of the home.

After their homes and the workshop were completed, the cousins had each turned their attentions to the projects they were most passionate about. For Mike that meant the restoration of the other structures on the property, and for JC it meant fortifying the property against the catastrophic event he felt certain was coming. While Mike started by getting to work on the castle, which he intended to house all the village's major operations and government offices, JC went about designing an elaborate wall that would encompass the entire perimeter of the town. In keeping with the medieval theme, he decided to put a moat around the exterior of the wall with a reinforced drawbridge being the main entrance into the town. In his eyes, not only did the moat preserve the medieval feel, but it was also one more measure of security. He considered building the wall and moat to average medieval specs but decided it might be overkill. There was no doubt it would be a big financial hit, but he still wanted them to present an extraordinary obstacle for whoever or whatever might pose a threat to their town. In the end he decided the moat would be made of reinforced concrete seven feet deep and twelve feet wide while the wall would be twenty feet tall and four feet thick and also made of reinforced concrete. To make the concrete more aesthetically pleasing he opted to cover it with a layer of thin stone.

The cousins installed sewer and solar power systems and erected a large farm at the back of the town with the intent of making the town as self-sustaining as possible. At JC's insistence, a series of underground facilities and panic rooms were put into place, all with the catastrophe he predicted in mind. Mike thought JC was being a bit paranoid and going overboard, but he was so thrilled to have JC working with him that he didn't attempt to rein him in. Besides, he thought the farm and solar power were good ideas. He even suggested adding some windmills citing they would be a good source of backup energy on top of being charming. By the time they completed the town a few years later it consisted of the castle, an eight acre farm, a small water treatment facility, the sewer system, the solar system, the windmills, the underground facilities, Mike's home, JC's home, a two acre lake, two restaurants, a theatre for plays and musical performances, a movie theatre, a park, a school, the workshop, a medical facility, a small ten unit apartment building, and thirty more houses of varying sizes.

JC and Mike began to look for residents to populate their town by mentioning it to like-minded friends and colleagues who ran in the same circles they did. It didn't take long for word to spread resulting in JC and Mike receiving calls from the likes of artists, writers, scientists, and computer wizzes to name a few. Dozens of people looking for a place to belong were excited to learn of this new town and eager to become part of it. The cousins began the process of screening prospective residents and decided the time had come to name their town. After much consideration they christened it Sandbox, a name that was tied to JC's love of gaming. In the world of gaming a sandbox game is pretty much unrestrictive, giving the player the freedom to explore and a great degree of creativity. JC found it fitting as they'd started the project with the goal of giving people a place to be creative, freely express themselves, and explore their chosen fields, much like a sandbox game.

With a name for their town, they welcomed their first new citizens, a thirty-year-old woman with artistic aspirations, a married couple comprised of a pianist and game developer along with their five-month-old son, and finally a graphic novelist who went by Hobo. Soon afterward they welcomed a middle-aged couple. The husband was a retired farmer who still enjoyed gardening, and the wife was from

NASA and was enjoying her retirement making candles. JC saw them as particularly valuable additions to Sandbox. From there the community continued to grow.

JC and Mike tried to spend as much time as they could in Sandbox getting to know their new community, but their lives and careers often kept them away for weeks on end. At the time of the outbreak in Roma, Arizona they hadn't had a chance to make it back to Sandbox in several months, so when JC arrived at Sandbox in the box truck with Mike, Capp, Gracie, Gray, Jordan, Tooter, and Giga in tow, he had to wonder what he was about to find inside. He had built Sandbox to withstand almost any threat, but he knew there was always the possibility of something going wrong in any situation. Despite his concerns, when he looked over to Capp and saw his jaw drop and the expression of awe on his face at his first glimpse of Sandbox, JC couldn't help but feel a sense of pride.

"Welcome home, Capp. Welcome to Sandbox."

Capp's jaw dropped as he gazed in awe upon the massive wall surrounding Sandbox with the top of the castle peeping over it. JC had told them all about Sandbox back in Florida. He'd told them how fortified it was to protect its citizens, but Capp had never imagined the true extent of it. "You and Mike financed all of this," Capp asked, the shock obvious in his voice.

"Yes, that's right."

Capp shook his head in amusement. "Man, I obviously chose the wrong career path."

JC simply smiled as he opened the driver's side door. "Sit tight for a second."

Capp watched JC walk to the front of the truck. JC's eyes were fixed on a space of the wall next to the drawbridge. Capp followed JC's gaze. At first glance, that area of the wall looked no different than any of the rest of the wall, but after straining his eyes for a bit, Capp realized there was an extremely thin laser light projecting from the area JC was focusing on. After standing there for a few seconds, JC let out an exasperated sigh.

JC stepped closer to the wall and looked into the tiny camera lens just above the laser motion sensor he'd installed years earlier. "GLaDIS?" After a brief pause with no response, he spoke more loudly. "GLaDIS, come on! I know you're probably mad at me, but it could be dangerous out here."

Capp wondered who JC was speaking to and rolled his window down so as to hear any response he got more clearly.

“Good,” a woman’s voice replied over an intercom.

The sound of her voice startled Capp. He hadn’t expected the unusual sound of her voice. She sounded almost robotic. Capp thought surely his ears couldn’t have heard what he thought they did. He decided to write it off as some sort of distortion in the intercom system.

“GLaDIS, come on! Please,” JC pled with the disembodied voice.

“Why should I, you monster,” GLaDIS retorted.

JC wanted to tell her what she could kiss, but he knew that would only reinforce her resolve to keep him out. He knew it would be better to play her game. He ducked his head sheepishly. “Look, I’m sorry, but I have others with me.”

“Others?”

“Yes, I have other people with me, including a child and two small dogs.”

GLaDIS was silent for a moment. When she finally responded the tone of her voice clearly gave away how begrudged she felt. “You should thank them.”

“For what?”

“Because they are the only reason you’re getting in, you monster.”

JC smiled and hurried back to the truck as the drawbridge began to lower.

Capp watched JC slide back into the driver’s seat. “I don’t know who she is, but GLaDIS seems to be a bit harsh."

JC rolled his eyes. "You have no idea."

The box truck rolled across the drawbridge with Gray, Jordan, and Tooter following in an old Ford pickup. Gray and Jordan took Sandbox in with awe as Gray steered the truck across the drawbridge and into the village.

"When JC told us about this place, I didn't picture this at all," Jordan commented quietly.

"Growing up not far from here, I knew about this place and saw pictures of it back when it was still in operation, but it looked nothing like this," Gray replied.

The castle was located a few yards just inside the walls, JC parked the box truck in front of it and motioned for Gray to park next to him. Several people rushed to greet them, many of them obviously delighted to see JC return to his beloved Sandbox. JC appeared to be equally delighted to see them. After exchanging warm greetings, hugs, and handshakes with them, JC proceeded to introduce Capp, Gracie, Gray, and Jordan to them as well as the dogs accompanying them, Giga and Tooter.

JC scanned the crowd. "I see some new faces here."

A voice from behind JC and his traveling companions offered an explanation for the new faces he saw in the crowd. "We had new residents move in after you left, and we took in survivors after the world went to shit."

They all turned to see a thin man with long hair and a long beard smiling at JC.

"Gentlemen, and little lady," JC began, making sure to include Gracie, "I'd like you to meet our very own Hobo Jesus."

"Just Hobo will be fine," the man informed them.

"I know you," Capp announced, "You streamed on Twitch, and we followed each other on Twitter."

Hobo blushed slightly. "I'm honored you remember, Capp. I've always been a fan of yours."

Capp extended his hand which Hobo immediately shook. "Nice to finally meet you."

"It really is a small world," Jordan mused.

Gracie, who'd been chatting with some of the children in the crowd, tugged on her father's arm. "Daddy, can I take Giga and Tooter to play with these kids. They said there are a couple of other dogs here and they have a playground."

Capp looked at his daughter and the children with her, all of them staring up at him with hopeful, pleading eyes. He wanted her to have friends her age and to be able to be a child, but having only gotten her back a short time before, he was hesitant, especially considering the state of the world they now lived in. "Well, honey, I can't make decisions about Tooter. That would be up to Gray. Besides, we just got here."

Picking up on Capp's concerns, Hobo tried to reassure him. "I promise, she's perfectly safe within these walls. Probably safer than she was even before the apocalypse."

"I think Tooter would enjoy it," Gray interjected.

Jordan spoke up. "I could use a little fun. I'll keep an eye on her, Capp."

Capp looked to Jordan, then back to his little girl. "Know what? I think you've earned some fun," he relented.

The child flung her arms around her father. "Thank

you, Daddy!" She then happily trotted off with the children of Sandbox, Jordan, Giga, and Tooter.

After the children were gone JC pulled Hobo to the side. He quietly told Hobo he was going to take the box truck to the ZRI lab and asked if the doors were unlocked. Hobo assured him they were and let him know a professor had a team of students doing research in the lab at that very moment. JC asked him to escort Capp and Gray over to the lab while he drove the truck over.

Hobo used the short walk to the lab as an opportunity to chat with Capp and Gray. He enjoyed getting to know them both a bit, but he couldn't help but notice there was no sign of Mike, and JC hadn't asked about him. It led Hobo to believe JC already knew of Mike's whereabouts and fate. Once they'd reached the lab and JC backed the box truck to the doors, Hobo considered asking about Mike but decided to wait until they'd squared away whatever JC wanted to do at the lab. With that in mind, Hobo joined the other three men at the back of the truck and immediately sensed a change in their demeanor as they stared in silence at the truck's roll-up door.

"You guys got a bomb or something in there," Hobo joked. The men turned to look at him in unison. The serious expressions on their faces unnerved him. "What's going on?"

"Do you think it's safe for the people here to know," Gray asked JC.

JC shook his head emphatically. "Absolutely not! They wouldn't understand. Their fear would override any reasoning."

Capp felt a need to defend the innate human nature of the people he'd met only moments before. "And that would be a perfectly natural reaction."

"Of course, it would be," JC responded. "However, you know the situation at hand and understand it, you understand why I am doing this. You know this must be done because you've been there from the beginning, which makes a difference. You've seen it all firsthand which is why you have been able to overcome that completely natural and understandable fear. The people here didn't have that opportunity which will make it harder for them to overcome it, and I fear it would lead to a very ugly and possibly violent situation. All of that having been said, we will have to trust a select few though." He turned to Hobo. "Which professor is in the lab?"

"Professor Jorgen," a bewildered Hobo answered.

The smile on JC's face told the others he was pleased by the answer. "Jorgen will understand the situation completely, and he can be trusted."

Gray motioned to Hobo. "What about him?"

JC didn't hesitate with his reply. "Without a doubt. Hobo proved himself to be invaluable and completely trustworthy to both me and Mike long ago." With that, he reached for the handle on the truck's roll-up door.

"Speaking of Mike," Hobo began, but before he could finish JC flung up the door. Inside Hobo saw something that caused him to take a few unsteady steps back. Horrified, he exclaimed, "You brought a zombie in here!"

"Take a closer look," JC instructed.

Hobo's instincts told him to kill it or run, but his mind told him JC would never put anyone in Sandbox in jeopardy. He decided to trust JC and slowly started to take timid steps forward, squinting into the dark interior of the truck's cargo bay. As he got closer to the creature in the truck, his eyes adjusted, allowing him to see that the creature was actually smiling. At that point his curiosity overrode his fear. He'd never seen one of them smile before. He continued to move forward. Once his eyes adjusted more, he was able to make out the features of the smiling face and was immediately overcome by feelings of shock and sadness. "Oh, no. Mike," he uttered.

"O-bo," Mike half grunted to the amazement of all four men.

"He... he... he..." Gray stammered.

Capp finished the sentence for him. "He spoke! He recognized him and said his name!"

JC's eyes sparkled. "He did indeed."

"Okay, guys, I'm really going to need an explanation here," Hobo demanded.

"You will get one," JC assured him. "First, we need Professor Jorgen to get his students out of the building, and we need to get Mike into a containment room. Then I will tell you and the professor the entire story."

Hobo reluctantly went inside. He told the professor that JC was back and needed to speak to him privately. Professor Jorgen told his students to put away their equipment and dismissed them. Hobo escorted the students out a door on the opposite end of the building, insuring they were well away from the contents of the box truck. Locking the door behind the students, he motioned for the professor to follow him. When they reached the door the truck was backed up to Hobo paused.

"Professor, I can't think of any way to prepare you for what you're about to see. The only thing I can do is tell you it is imperative you stay calm, trust JC, and don't draw any attention in our direction. Got it?"

The professor was puzzled. "You've aroused my curiosity, but I will do as you have instructed."

Hobo opened the door. Upon stepping out Professor Jorgen saw JC and two men he didn't recognize. He also saw a truck containing a zombie he did recognize. He didn't jump back, gasp, or run. He remained perfectly calm. "Oh my," was his only reaction.

The professor and Hobo helped JC, Capp, and Gray get Mike into the building as quickly and quietly as possible. To their relief, it seemed no one took notice of their activity. Once Mike was safely strapped to a chair in one corner of the containment room Hobo and Professor Jorgen couldn't tear their eyes away from him. They cautiously circled him and marveled at how calm and alert he was. The usual frenzied, mindless aggression they'd witnessed from other zombies was nowhere to be found in Mike. Rather, he sat quite calmly and still in his chair, save for the random twitch of a limb or slight jerk of his head. He didn't wear the usual blank stare of others in his condition. In its place was a smile and the distinct look of recognition emanating from his eyes. If not for the discoloration of his skin and slight yet obvious smell of decomposition, they would have thought him to be a fully living, functioning human being.

"How did this happen," Professor Jorgen probed.

Capp smirked. "You should probably take a seat for this."

"Rest assured I can handle whatever you are about to tell me," the professor replied indignantly.

JC cleared his throat. "Professor, Capp meant nothing disparaging about your strength or character. I believe he was referring to the fact it is a very long story."

Upon hearing that the professor thought it was perhaps best if the story were told over a meal. JC, Capp, and Gray couldn't deny they were hungry after their long journey from Florida. Professor Jorgen told them one of the couples who lived in Sandbox had made an exceptionally large pot of stew to feed everyone for the day.

"Make yourselves comfortable while Hobo and I fetch some stew and sweet tea."

Hobo nodded, "And I'll make sure Gracie and Jordan get some too."

After Jorgen and Hobo left Gray turned to JC, "How much are you going to tell them?"

JC was confused by the question. "All of it of course."

"Including the work you and Mike were doing for the government," Gray pressed.

JC nodded. "I will indeed."

Capp was concerned. "Aren't you afraid of their reaction or that they may tell the others? I have a feeling they might react even worse to that than you worried they would over Mike. It could go very badly."

JC thought it over for a moment before responding. "As for Hobo and the good professor, I have not one doubt they can be trusted and will understand what Mike and I were doing. As for everyone else, I agree with you. I know Hobo and Jorgen won't tell them, and I don't believe any of us should either. Some of them won't understand the work we were doing or what we are currently attempting to do with Mike. We should wait until we have more research and progress to show them."

Other than a few grunts and groans from Mike, the room fell into an uncomfortable silence. Gray and Capp were both contemplating the same question, but neither wanted to be the one to ask it. They knew JC loved Mike and that the entire situation had been hard on him. Neither of them wanted to cause him more pain, but Gray finally decided the question had to be asked.

His voice heavy with sympathy, Gray asked, "Realistically, do you think Mike will make progress?"

JC gazed at his cousin with both love and pain. "He as to," he muttered.

The door opened, and the professor and Hobo wheeled in a cart loaded with bowls, spoons, napkins, glasses, bread, crackers, a pot of stew, and a pitcher of sweet tea. The professor set about sterilizing a lab table while Hobo gathered stools.

Hobo gestured for the men to take a seat around the table. "Dinner is served, gentlemen."

They ate and conversed about a variety of topics; mainly what JC had missed during his time away from Sandbox. Had they not been in a lab with a zombified Mike sitting just a few feet away it would have been much like any normal gathering of old friends. However, Professor Jorgen was acutely aware it wasn't a normal gathering and didn't intend to let anyone forget that.

Jorgen dabbed at the corners of his mouth with a napkin. "JC not to be rude, but enough chit-chat. How did Mike end up in this condition, and why is he not like the others?"

JC sighed. "That's a fair question. I could give you the short, simple explanation, but I respect you too much for that. You deserve the complete story, from the beginning."

JC inhaled sharply. "As you already know, I was a bioengineer, and Mike and I both worked for the Biological Warfare and Disease Control Division of the Department of Defense. I specialized in disease control, prevention, and treatment. In Chile I was considered top in my field. When the U.S. found itself deep in conflict with another country and on the verge of war, some government officials sought the help of some of the top scientists around the world to develop a defense against a biological weapon they feared might be used against their troops." He paused to take a sip of his tea and collect his thoughts.

JC continued to explain he had been approached to work on that defense but had refused on the basis biological warfare went against his core beliefs. Several scientists had accepted though, including another from Chile. His name was Louis Russo, and JC had worked with him in the past. Russo arrogantly considered himself to be the most brilliant scientist of his generation and felt he had not been shown the respect and admiration he deserved. He'd seen the invitation from the U.S. as a way to obtain that respect and admiration. He'd dug into the project with passion. However, he'd soon decided the best defense would be a better offense. Operating under that theory, he'd developed a highly contagious and deadly virus meant to alter brain function, making victims docile and submissive.

As brilliant as Russo was, his arrogance prevented him from realizing he'd made some devastating mistakes. Due to his miscalculations the virus actually resulted in death with a strange brain mutation occurring shortly after. The result of that mutation had been the zombies, or the afflicted as Capp's and Gray's group had called them. After learning of this, the U.S. government had promptly pulled the plug on the project and ordered everything associated with Russo's research and virus to be destroyed, but before the order could be carried out, an enraged Russo had managed to slip away with most of his research and work, including a sample of the virus. A highly classified task force had been formed to find him and a new team of scientists assembled to develop a counter to the virus which had been nicknamed the Resurrection Bug, or R-Bug for short.

It had been then that Mike reached out to JC on behalf of the BWDCD, who had been warned of the Russo situation and was frantically working with the new team to head off a possible disaster. Mike's plea worked, JC decided to help, partially due to the great love and respect he had for his cousin but also because he knew the potential worldwide devastation the R-Bug could cause. While JC and the others fervently worked on the development of an antivirus, the task force worked around the clock to locate Russo. During their search they learned he had always felt some resentment towards the U.S. because his father had abandoned him and his mother for an American woman when Russo was six. He also harbored a strong dislike for the retail giant, Danterford's.

Danterford's stores were big box superstores that came in two varieties, Danterford's Emporiums and Danterford's Mega Centers. At a Danterford's Emporium a customer could easily buy groceries, clothing, pet supplies, housewares, and gas among a few other things. While the Emporiums were impressive the Mega Centers were the ultimate middle class shopping experience; complete one-stop shopping for just about anything one's heart could desire. Danterford's Mega Centers offered everything the Emporiums did and more, including a restaurant, lumber, building supplies, automotive repairs, and a gun shop. The Mega Centers also housed the warehouses for Danterford's Wholesale Distribution. Over the years Danterford's had been the target of two activist groups. One blamed the retail giant for the downfall of countless mom and pop businesses, and the other believed Danterford's didn't pay their employees a fair living wage. Both groups had regularly expressed their disapproval of the company through vandalism and theft at several of the chain's locations, forcing the company to up their security measures, such as putting tall fences around their stores, particularly the Mega Centers.

Such large operations required the acquisition of large parcels of land. The retail chain had begun to expand internationally just a couple of years before the incident that would bring the world to its knees and create the afflicted. They'd decided to open two locations in Chile as part of their expansion efforts. Around that same time Russo's mother was struggling financially. She'd never really been able to stabilize her life or finances after her husband had abandoned them, but she had managed to keep them fed and hold onto their land which had been in her family for generations. Life had another blow in store for her though, she was diagnosed with cancer. She'd continued to work, but inevitably her condition deteriorated, rendering her unable to carry out the duties of her job. Once she had to leave her job it wasn't long before she was so far behind on her bills there was no way she'd ever be able to catch up. Her pride wouldn't allow her to ask anyone for help, especially her son. Soon creditors were calling day and night, and some sent men out to repossess things. When Danterford's approached her with an offer to buy her land she felt she had no choice but to accept, despite the fact it was for only half of what the property was worth. Naturally, Louis Russo had been infuriated when he found out. His father's abandonment for an American woman, an American company taking advantage of his sick mother, and finally the American government's refusal to recognize the brilliance of his virus all combined to ignite in Louis Russo a raging hatred of the United States of America.

Once the task force learned all of those things, they realized exactly how volatile he could possibly be, but the information had also given them clues as to where to start looking for the unhinged scientist. Those clues led them to one of the extremist groups that had targeted Danterford's. What better place for an angry madman to hide than among others as outraged as he was? The task force reached out to the FBI, who had been tracking the group for quite some time. Together they'd tracked Russo and the group to Arizona. Danterford's two biggest locations were located in Washington, D.C. and Phoenix, Arizona. Russo had convinced the group that the best way to punish both Danterford's and the United States government for all the evils they believed them to be guilty of was to release the R-Bug, but he lied to them about the true consequences of releasing the deadly virus. He told them it could be contained to a targeted area and would die before it could spread outside of the area; neither was true. With the help of the misguided group Russo originally planned to release the R-Bug at the Danterford's location in D.C., effectively taking out one Danterford's biggest locations as well as many government officials, but he'd assumed the task force hunting him would be expecting that, so he changed course. He decided the best idea would be to release the R-Bug at several Danterford's locations across the country, starting with the Phoenix location, but then he learned there would be a convention in a city not far from Phoenix, and he saw a golden opportunity.

The Streamers and Creators Convention was an annual affair held in Roma, Arizona. The event celebrated streamers and creators from two of the most popular platforms on the internet, Twitch and YouTube. Both platforms had become essential to many online personalities, including gamers. Twitch afforded streamers the chance to interact on a more personal level with their fans while YouTube allowed creators the opportunity to upload prerecorded videos to their channels to keep their fans engaged. The convention gave streamers, creators, and fans a place to come together in person. It was a place for them to meet, chat, play games, and get news about upcoming games. It was quite a big deal, especially within the gaming community.

Russo decided to have the activist group release R-Bug at the Phoenix Danterford's location and the convention simultaneously, swiftly followed by releases across the country. He convinced them to go along with targeting the convention by pointing out Danterford's sponsored it and several of Danterford's board members would be there. What he did not tell them was the board members were only part of his motivation for the attack in Roma. He knew some government officials were also going to be in attendance to promote a campaign for less violence in video games. The campaign had come in the wake of a rash of school shootings for which many officials insisted video games were partially to blame. Russo saw the fact gamers from around the world would also be there as a bonus. His hope was an attack that affected those gamers would serve to anger other countries or at the very least cause them to deem the United States unsafe thereby making them less likely to send any aid to the United States.

The task force had placed resources and military personnel at both the DC and Phoenix Danterford's locations. Mike and JC had been sent to the Phoenix location where they were to attempt to contain and neutralize the virus should Russo be captured in Arizona while another team of scientists awaited to attempt the same thing in Washington, DC if he was captured there. Government officials had warned Danterford's there was a possible threat, but in an effort to prevent causing a panic or the true severity of the situation being leaked to the public they told Danterford's there was threat of a protest they felt could hold the potential for some violence and property damage. While not exactly a lie, it wasn't exactly the truth either. The government assured Danterford's they would be watching and prevent things from becoming violent. They requested Danterford's leave both locations open and carry on with business as usual with the hope of not alerting Russo and the activists to anything being amiss. However, Danterford's executives felt there was more to the story than they were being told and decided they weren't willing to risk their employees' safety and closed both locations. The task force had been certain the closings would be a red flag to Russo and prompt him to abandon any plans he had to attack the locations. When nothing happened in DC, they'd taken it as confirmation they'd been right. Assuming the threat had subsided for the time being, they pulled all scientists and military from both locations.

Having known Russo for quite some time, JC hadn't believed he would abandon his devious plans so easily. JC believed Russo's ego would never allow him to do that. In light of that belief, JC and Mike felt Russo might target the convention and had opted to stay in Arizona against orders. The way they'd viewed it was if they were wrong, which they'd hoped they were, they would at least have a chance to enjoy the convention. In JC's mind that scenario would have been a win-win, particularly considering he was an avid gamer and a YouTube creator himself. Upon being told of JC's and Mike's decision to stay the task force had basically told them to do as they pleased, but they would not leave any resources or manpower behind to help them as they saw no reason to believe their theory about the convention was valid. As it turned out JC's and Mike's instincts had been spot-on. The closing of the Phoenix Danterford's location hadn't deterred Ruso and his merry band of misguided activists at all. They'd proceeded with their plans at the convention along with various Danterford's locations across the country. Although JC and Mike had been fully aware of how dangerous R-Bug was they hadn't known exactly how quickly it affected its victims, and with what few resources they'd personally brought with them, they'd been powerless to do anything.

Hobo and Jorgen were appalled by what they were hearing, but not necessarily surprised. Neither man trusted any government or organized religion, believing too many individuals used both as justification for hate, to abuse and control others, or simply to feed their own greed and lust for power. Both men had been called conspiracy theorists and things of the like many times in their lives so, JC's story, while horrific, made them feel almost vindicated.

"To speed this up a little," JC continued, "we eventually came across Games4Kickz, Kage848, Starsnipe, and several others in Phoenix, including Capp and Gray here. We all traveled together to a military base in Florida. I'd thought we might find it still secure and inhabited." His voice trailed off as he added, "I was wrong."

Jorgen leaned in to pat JC's hand. "I know you must have seen horrifying things. For that, my heart goes out to you, but it still doesn't explain how Mike came to be in his current state."

"It happened because he was trying to do the right thing," Capp interjected.

Gray nodded his head slowly. "Along the way to Florida we came across a mixed up and distraught teenage boy in Texas who was about to get himself eaten by several afflicted. Mike helped save him but was bitten in the process."

Jorgen slumped back on his stool. He opened his mouth as if he was going to say something, but nothing came out.

"My... My... My God," Hobo stammered. "Honestly, if anyone else were to tell me this story I wouldn't believe it."

Capp grinned. "We haven't even told you about Hope yet."

Hobo threw his hands in the air. "Who the hell is Hope?"

JC shook his head. "Not now. I will tell you, just not now. I think we've overloaded your minds enough for today."

"At least tell us what happened to Kickz and the others! Oh, and why you call them afflicted," Hobo pleaded.

"Well," Gray began, "Kickz started the afflicted thing. His train of thought was they used to be just like us. They had lives, families, friends, jobs, hobbies, all of that stuff, then one day they were hit with this thing that took it all away. It's much like when someone gets a disease such as cancer or diabetes; they didn't do anything to cause it or to deserve it, they were just afflicted with it." He motioned toward Mike. "They didn't cause this or deserve it, there were afflicted with it."

Once again, the men fell silent as the impact of that explanation and the weight of JC's story hit them. Hobo and Professor Jorgen tried to wrap their minds around it all while JC's, Capp's, and Gray's minds were flooded with memories.

Hobo cleared his throat, breaking the silence. “What about Kickz and the others?”

JC smiled softly. “We left them safe and sound in Florida a few days ago."

“As safe and sound as anyone can be these days anyway,” Capp added. “As we speak, they are securing and rebuilding a small town. There has been a lot of discussion about rebuilding society, one small town or settlement at a time.”

That statement piqued Professor Jorgen’s attention. “So, you all believe there are more survivors out there?”

“We know there is,” Capp stated. “We found some on the way to Florida. Besides that, if we all survived others must have too. We have to start rebuilding somewhere, preparing places for those survivors. Why not a small town in Florida?”

“Or a medieval village in Virginia.” JC grinned.

Capp nodded. “Exactly! The rebuilding of this country, and quite possibly this world, will start with people like us in places like this.”

Hobo’s face gave away the concern he was feeling. “It’s a wonderful thought, but how can this country ever be rebuilt with millions of afflicted roaming everywhere?”

Jorgen decided to field that question. “As far as we know, they are dead tissue. It stands to reason they will decompose. Even putting decomposition aside, there is the starvation factor. Survivors will, hopefully, continue to survive and avoid becoming a meal. The afflicted will run out of food. It is inevitable.”

JC gazed at Mike who managed to give him a twisted

smile. “There are always the options of a cure or evolution as well. Mike and a baby named Hope will be the keys to those options.”

Although Hobo still had many questions JC assured him he would get all the answers in due time. In an effort to quell Hobo's curiosity and concerns JC convinced him to take Gray on a tour of Sandbox. As they left the lab Gray could see Hobo was a bit sullen.

"Show me the kingdom," Gray cheerfully exclaimed in an attempt to raise Hobo's spirits, but the attempt proved to be unsuccessful.

"Why doesn't he trust me," Hobo asked, his tone heavy with hurt and frustration.

Gray abruptly stopped walking and placed his hand on Hobo's shoulder to stop him as well. "Man, Hobo, it's nothing like that. You've got it all wrong."

"Do I?"

"Yes, you do. In fact, Capp and I were worried about trusting you and the professor. We let JC know that too. He immediately informed us he had complete faith you would understand what we were doing and why we were doing it. He told us he had no doubt you could be trusted. I think right now he is just focused on keeping others from finding out, getting to work, and dealing with his own feelings about it all. It's obvious the people here trust you so, the more you're seen around Sandbox acting normal and calm the better the chances are folks won't start to get suspicious."

Hobo took a moment to think over Gray's explanation.

In his mind, it made sense. “Okay, I get it. I’ll admit, it makes me feel better.”

Gray relaxed. “I’ll tell you something else, me and JC have had our differences, but I’ve grown to trust him and his judgement. If he trusts you, well I trust you and look forward to getting to know you.”

A bashful grin spread across Hobo’s bearded face. “If we’re going to keep suspicions down and make you part of this community, we’d better get to introducing you to everybody.”

The sun had just gone down. The night air was crisp and cool but not chilly. The smell of Virginia pines wafted in on a gentle breeze. Gray soaked it all in, suddenly realizing how much he’d missed his home state. The night air, the stars, and the uniqueness of Sandbox combined to add a touch of magic to everything around them. As they strolled through the streets of Sandbox Hobo pointed out all the important public buildings along with the private homes and explained who lived in each. Along the way they encountered many citizens of Sandbox whom Hobo promptly introduced to Gray.

First there was thirty-year-old Rachel, a friendly artist with a bubbly personality and a touch of a hippie vibe. Then there was Bobby and Clara, a middle-aged couple who’d been married for nearly thirty years. Bobby was a retired farmer who still very much enjoyed growing things while Clara was retired from NASA and now spent her time making candles. There was also forty-year-old Lawrence who used to be a chemist and chief scientific officer at a large pharmaceutical company.

There was Lawrence, who was friendly enough, but once they were out of his earshot Hobo told Gray Lawrence's story. Lawrence, his wife, and their daughter, Shyla, had moved to Sandbox shortly after Hobo had. Lawrence's wife had been a doctor so, once Russo released his virus her first instinct was to help as many people as possible. She'd often made trips out to the main roads to find survivors, offering them food, water, medical attention, and shelter. Many accepted the food, water, and medical attention, but most declined her invitation to Sandbox, usually citing attempts to find family members as the reason. On one of her excursions, she'd found a mother and her two daughters, one of whom had been bitten by one of the afflicted. Lawrence's wife had swiftly brought them back to Sandbox as she'd felt the girl's wound would be better treated with the resources at her small office. At the time none of them knew a bite would turn someone into one of the afflicted. She worked frantically to treat the wound and bring down the girl's quickly rising fever, but it was to no avail, the girl died within hours. The heartbroken mother cradled her dead child and rocked her as she sobbed. She was still cradling the child when, a few minutes later, the girl began to jerk and groan. Lawrence's wife had been stunned while the mother had proclaimed it a miracle, but when the girl looked up at her mother she didn't look quite right. They'd realized the groan was in fact a growl mere seconds before the child sunk her teeth into her mother's jugular. Lawrence's wife had quickly pulled the girl off, flung her across the room, and tried to stop the mother's bleeding. As she did, the girl had bound back over to her and bit her arm.

Hobo sighed. "Poor woman managed to get her off her and get out of the room but realized in that moment what the bites did. She barricaded the door then sought out Lawrence and Bobby. They went with her back to her office where they found the little girl eating her mother's leg. Then her mother started to twitch. None of them were happy about it, but they knew what had to be done, and Lawrence and Bobby did it."

"What happened to Lawrence's wife?"

"No one had noticed the bite on her arm. When she asked for a few minutes alone with her husband they all assumed she was just shaken up and needed some comfort. Once she was alone with Lawrence, she told him the full story and showed him the bite on her arm. She told him she loved him and asked him to tell Shyla she was sorry and loved her too. Before he could really comprehend what was happening, she took a scalpel and rammed it into her right eye."

Gray was taken aback. He couldn't imagine being in either person's shoes. Who had it worse? The man who had to watch his wife die, or the woman forced to stab her own brain in order to protect the husband and daughter she loved? He was quietly pondering that question when another one crossed his mind. "What happened to the little girl's sister? You said the woman had two daughters. What happened to the other one?"

"I'll show you. We can check in on Jordan and Gracie while we're at it."

Hobo led Gray to a building that had a whimsical feel

about it. It was in keeping with the medieval theme of Sandbox but was painted in brighter colors with a few fairy tale murals on the outside walls. Gray noticed a small playground occupied the same parcel of land the building sat on, and he could hear children's laughter coming from inside. Hobo explained it was a school that served kids from preschool through high school graduation. They walked through the main lobby, turned left, and followed that hallway to the end where Hobo ushered Gray into a classroom where several children were playing. All the children appeared to be between the ages of five to seven years old. They were happy, healthy, and clean. If Gray hadn't known better he would have thought he was in the classroom of any normal school before the world ended. Hobo motioned toward a small, dark-haired girl with big, sad, brown eyes. She was the only child who wasn't playing or laughing. The sadness radiating from that small girl hit Gray like a ton of bricks. It had such an impact on him it took a minute for him to realize she was stroking something in her lap as she sat cross-legged on the floor. To his surprise, Tooter was curled up in the child's lap. He seemed completely content while she seemed as if she felt no one else was in the room other than herself and the tiny dog.

"When she was brought here with her mother and sister Lawrence's wife asked Shyla to look after her while she treated her sister," Hobo explained. "Shyla could see how scared the little girl was and brought her here thinking playing with other kids would make her feel better. Physically she was safe, but nothing could spare either her or Shyla from the emotional trauma of what happened. Neither of them has been quite right since. Her name is Maria."

"So, who takes care of her now?"

"A woman named Alice. Alice was another of the doctor's rescues. The doctor brought her here about three weeks before Maria and her family. Alice never intended to stay. She had a broken and infected leg among other injuries. Her plan was to stay long enough to heal and then go in search of her own kids somewhere in Arizona. A few days before she'd planned to leave someone passing through told her Arizona had been hit hard and there were no survivors. As you would expect, Alice was devastated. She sunk into such a deep depression we became worried she might be suicidal. Then Maria showed up. The two of them gravitated to each other. Maria snapped Alice out of her depression, and although Maria isn't exactly normal or happy, she's still better than she was. She's getting there. I think she feels safe with Alice at least, that's a start."

When a woman Gray assumed was a teacher called Hobo from across the room Gray told him to go ahead. He stayed behind, watching the girl for a moment longer before making his way over to her. "Hi, Maria." He squatted next to her. "I'm Gray. Seems like you and my little buddy, Tooter, are getting along good."

The girl never raised her eyes to look at him. She kept them focused on Tooter and continued to stroke his back. When she spoke, her voice was frail with a touch of fear in it. "I didn't take him, I promise. There was a boy in here, he came with the boy and just ran right to me. I didn't take him. The boy said I could play with him for a while. I didn't mean no harm."

"Oh, I know that. It's fine." Gray made it a point to keep his voice gentle and reassuring yet cheery. "It's a good thing Tooter found you. Know why?" Maria raised her eyes slightly. "Because he really likes little girls. How old are you?"

"Six."

Gray feigned astonishment. "Seriously? Well, no wonder he ran to you! Six is Tooter's favorite age! He loves all kids but especially six-year-olds!"

Maria fully raised her head to look at him. "Tooter's cool, but Gray is a funny name."

Gray chuckled. "I can't argue with that. My name is really Pete. Gray is sort of a nickname."

"I like Pete, but I like Gray too, even though it is funny." Maria looked down at Tooter then back up to Gray. "You should take him now. Alice will be here to get me soon." She gingerly lifted the small dog from her lap and gave him to Gray. "Will you guys be living here now?"

"Yeah, I suppose we will be. We're going to be around for quite a while anyway."

Maria seemed more at ease as she got to her feet. "If Alice says it's okay, can Tooter come to our house and play sometimes?"

"I don't see why not. I think Tooter would like that. See that guy over there? The guy named Hobo? Do you know him?"

Maria nodded. "Everybody here knows him. His name is funny too, but he's nice."

Gray snickered. "I will have that nice man show me where your house is so I can stop by to ask Alice."

The girl's eyes brightened, she gave a quick nod, patted

Tooter's head, and then dashed off to the other side of the room to gather her things.

Hobo, who was making his way back over to Gray, gave Maria a little wave. He smiled as Gray stood up. "Looks like Alice isn't the only one who can make a connection with Maria."

"Yeah, Tooter seems to have a knack with her," Gray laughed. "She said Tooter came in here with a boy, I'm guessing that was Jordan, but where is he now?" Where's Gracie?"

"They're down the hall. The teacher said Jordan is really good with kids. She was surprised to find out he was twenty. She thought he was around fourteen. I suppose he does look pretty young for his age. Hell, I would have pegged him for fifteen or sixteen. I didn't know he was twenty until she told me."

"He doesn't look his age," Gray agreed. "It's more than that though. He has almost a childlike innocence about him that makes him seem younger. At the same time, there's also an intelligence about him that gives him an air of wisdom beyond his years. I've always thought there was a lot going on inside him. He's a good kid though."

"Things should be as close to normal as possible for him as well as comfortable. He is clearly displaying obvious signs of his memory and humanity still being somewhat intact. Normal and comfortable may help encourage that," JC passionately explained as Professor Jorgen examined Mike. "Also, it will make me feel better to know he is comfortable."

Jorgen prepared to draw blood samples from Mike. "From a scientific standpoint it makes perfect sense. From a human standpoint it also makes perfect sense."

Capp cleared his throat. "From either standpoint the most logical place to achieve normal and comfortable would be in his home. He did have his own home here, didn't he?"

Jorgen was listening to the other two men but continued with the task at hand. "Okay, Mike, I have to take a little bit of blood now. Do you remember ever having this done in the past?" Mike nodded slowly. "Good. Very good. I will be as gentle as possible."

"Yes, he has a home here," JC answered to Capp's question. "I agree that would be the best place, but how do we get him there without attracting the attention of the entire village? Even if we pulled that off, how would we explain the activity going on at his house afterward?"

"Here we go," Jorgen quietly warned before swiftly and gently easing the needle into Mike's arm. Mike's face distorted into a scowl. A nonhuman growl escaped him, alarming both JC and Capp. Jorgen, however, remained calm and steady as he continued to draw the blood. "Oh, hush now. No need for all of that. We're almost done."

JC and Capp held their breath as they watched closely for Mike's next reaction. Capp marveled at Professor Jorgen's apparent nerves of steel. Mike's growl dissipated and was replaced by a whimper. The scowl on Mike's face transformed into a look of fear and pain. His lip quivered slightly. Capp noticed he resembled a scared little boy.

JC must have noticed it too because he rushed over to take Mike's hand in his. "It's to help you, cousin," JC whispered. Mike responded by tenderly squeezing JC's hand.

Jorgen finished up. "There we go, Mike. All done."

"Is he good to be moved," Capp inquired of Jorgen.

"I believe he is."

"What do you have in mind," JC asked.

Before Capp could answer, the lab door opened quite unexpectedly causing everyone, including Mike, to jump. They were relieved to see it was Gray and Hobo returning with Jordan and Grace in tow.

"How are things going," Gray asked.

"Well, Mike has been a splendid patient," Jorgen reported.

Capp stared at Mike. "He was, all things considered. It's amazing how he manages to control the afflicted urges he must be feeling."

"Yes, but as we were just discussing, the best place for him, as well as for our purposes, would be in his home here in Sandbox. We just have to get home over there without alerting the entire village of his presence," JC fretted.

Jordan started digging through his backpack. "For starters, he needs some clean clothes on, preferably some that hide his face and skin." He pulled a pair of jeans and a black hoodie from his backpack. "Something like these."

Grace nodded in approval, then opened her backpack. "Jordan has the right idea, but he could use a little freshening up too." She glanced at Mike. "Sorry, but you do have a little bit of a funk going on." She retrieved body wash and shampoo from her backpack and sat them on a table before also pulling out a pair of sunglasses and a makeup bag. “These should help disguise any parts of his face the hoodie doesn’t completely hide.”

Capp wrinkled his nose. “Why do you have makeup? You’re not old enough for that!”

Grace huffed. “Chill, Dad!”

Capp baulked. “Excuse me!”

“Dad, I haven’t been wearing it, but I have been collecting it and practicing with it. We’re in the middle of an apocalypse, who knows if manufacturers will ever reopen, and makeup does go bad. I figured if I don’t get it now, I may never have a chance to know what it’s like to use it.”

Capp’s mood instantly changed. His daughter’s words stung because they were true. He felt a sadness knowing his daughter even had to think along those lines, but he felt and even greater sadness over the fact her mother wasn’t around to teach her how to use the makeup she’d collected. “Do you like it?”

“I think so, but I’m not very good at it yet.”

He smiled at her. “I’m sure you’ll get better.”

“Jordan, my boy, grab those bath products,” Jorgen instructed. “Gray, JC, help me get Mike down to the decontamination shower. Young lady, set up your cosmetics and prepare to practice your skills.”

Jorgen, Gray, JC, and Jordan picked Mike up, still strapped to his chair, and made their way to the shower. Hobo followed closely behind them after gathering some towels. Capp and Grace were left behind in the lab.

Grace happily went about laying her makeup, brushes,

and sponges out on a table. Capp watched her, glad to see his daughter have the opportunity to do something that made her smile. It was something almost normal in a world that was anything but. The almost part put a damper on the moment for Capp. He seriously doubted any other little girl in the world had ever given an afflicted a makeover. Although he was amazed by how well Mike was doing, he was concerned about Grace being so close to him.

Capp picked up a sponge Grace had placed on the table. "Funny looking thing," he observed. "What's it for?"

"It's a beauty blender, Daddy. You blend foundation with it."

Capp pursed his lips and inspected the blender a little closer. "If you say so." He put the blender back in its place. "Are you comfortable with this, honey? If you're not, that's okay. Everyone will understand."

Grace ran her fingers down the handle of a brush on the table. "Actually, I'm not." She raised her eyes to meet her father's gaze. "I know Mike has been doing very good. I know he is different from the other afflicted, he really is, and I know he would never want to purposely hurt me or anyone else. I also know he may not be able to stop himself." Capp opened his mouth to speak, but she held her hand up to silence him. "Daddy, I still want to do it. Yes, I am nervous, but I have to do it. Right now we all have to do things we are uncomfortable with. Mike was a good person, and he is still in there somewhere. Plus, he may be the answer to saving other people. I want to be part of helping him and others in any way I can."

Capp couldn't argue with her, she had valid points, but he was caught off guard by the maturity and selflessness his beautiful girl was displaying. He knew adults who weren't capable of what the child in front of him was. He'd always been proud of her, but in that moment, he'd never been prouder.

In the shower the group of men debated how best to undress and bathe Mike.

"We have to unstrap him from that chair," Jordan insisted.

The men stood over Mike in a circle. Mike quietly looked up at them with a twisted grin.

Jorgen smiled back at him. "I believe the lad is right. There simply isn't any other way."

Hobo was obviously hesitant about the whole situation. "What if he bites us?"

JC shared Hobo's concerns. "I love Mike, but we can't take the chance. If we had something to use as a muzzle perhaps..."

Gray cut him short. "No, that's not right! We're trying to get through to whatever humanity he still has inside. How are we supposed to accomplish that if we're muzzling him like a dog? I'm not saying we shouldn't be cautious; we'd be crazy not to be, but we have been. We've kept him restrained even though he has given us no indication he will hurt us. I understand why we do it, but what kind of message does that send to him? And now we're talking about muzzling him?"

The group mulled over what Gray said as they stared down at Mike, who continued to look up at them with his twisted smile. Without warning, Jordan quickly freed one of Mike's arms. The others gasped; Mike raised his hand to watch his fingers wiggle.

"For Christ's sake, the boy has more balls than all of you," GLaDIS blurted.

The sound of her voice startled them all. They'd almost forgotten about her.

Hobo rolled his eyes. "Have you been listening this whole time, GLaDIS?"

"Of course I have. I've been watching too."

JC stepped in "GLaDIS, it is imperative that no one else in the village knows of this." He received no response. "GLaDIS," he coaxed.

"I'm not an idiot," GLaDIS retorted. "If this were only about you, you monster, I would alert them right away and watch gleefully while they put you to death. Unfortunately, I have others to consider. For that reason, I will keep your secret, but please, grow a pair! Jordan and Gray are right."

"We do have enough of us here we should be able to contain him," Hobo reasoned.

"I don't think we'll have to worry about that." Jordan held his hand out to Mike who gently took it in his own.

Mike's twisted grin grew wider. Jordan helped him to his feet, and suddenly his eyes seemed more alive. They looked as if they were close to twinkling.

Capp and Grace were in the middle of a round of Phase 10 when the group returned from the shower. Their mouths gapped open when they saw a freshly showered

Mike unrestrained and walking toward them. Seeing concern on Capp's face JC rushed ahead of Mike. He pulled Capp aside and quickly explained what had taken place in the shower and their reasoning for setting him free.

Capp looked past JC to the afflicted Mike who was now only a couple of feet away from his daughter. "I get it. I really get it, but that is my child."

JC pulled his knife from its sheath on his belt. "I will put him down myself before I let him hurt her."

Capp reluctantly gave in.

The interaction between the two men did not escape the attention of the observant Grace. "It's okay, Daddy." She then turned her attention to Mike. She gave the seat in front of the cosmetics table a pat. "Have a seat, Mr. Mike. I'm going to try to help you look a little more like yourself."

Mike moved to the chair with clumsy jerking motions and sat down. He was looking at Grace's cosmetics when a small mirror amid them caught his attention. He picked it up, fumbling with it for a moment before finally managing to turn it toward him. An alarmed grunt escaped him. He touched his cheek then began to grunt, growl, and stomp the floor. JC readied his knife. Capp rushed to position himself between Mike and Grace, but Grace was not having it. She sidestepped her father to stand between Mike and JC. She knelt in front of Mike and placed her hand on his knee. Mike looked down at her and stopped stomping but continued to grunt and growl.

Grace raised her finger to her lips. "Shh. Calm down, please, Mr. Mike. I want to tell you something, but you have to be calm to hear it."

Mike got very still and quiet. He gazed down at her with wide eyes full of sorrow.

"There you go. That's much better." Grace gently stroked his cheek. "You've been through so much, and I am so very sorry for that. I wish I could take away all the bad for you, but I can't. What I can do is be your friend. As your friend I can help you look more like you used to and help you learn how to do things again. While I do that your other friends here can work on a way to help make you better. None of it will be easy, and there will be times you will feel sad and frustrated, just like you do right now, but it will be worth it, and we will be with you every step of the way. All you have to do is try your very best to do what we tell you and to control how you handle your frustration. Is it okay if we do that? Can you do that?"

Mike smiled and tenderly patted her cheek with his trembling hand. Grace took that as a yes and set about her work. All of the men stood close by, ready to defend Grace if need be, with the exception of Professor Jorgen. He sat at a table nearby, scribbling notes about Mike's behavior and reactions on his clipboard while a video camera he'd set up captured every moment. Twenty minutes later Grace finished. She informed them it wasn't perfect, but it was the best she could do.

Jorgen moved in to get a closer look at Mike. "My dear girl, I think you did a tremendous job!"

Jordan agreed. "Totally! He looks more human now. Maybe a human who has been a little sick and exhausted but not so much like one of the afflicted. Considering what you had to work with, I'd say that is an incredible improvement." As soon as the words left his mouth, he regretted the way he'd worded his statement. "Sorry, Mike. I didn't mean any offense."

Mike reached for the mirror which Jordan handed him. He tilted his head from side to side while examining his reflection.

Jorgen wrote vigorously on his clipboard. "Extraordinary."

Continuing to look at his reflection, Mike smiled.

Moments later the entire group was making their way to Mike's house, struggling to look as normal and casual as possible. Mike was in the center of the group with Grace and Jordan on either side of him. Grace held his hand while Jordan tried to covertly steady him as he walked. The shadows of the night, the hoodie, and Grace's makeup worked together wonderfully. As long as no one got too close to him they'd never know anything was wrong with him. The group walked in a manner that would seem to most as simply a group of friends out for a stroll and chatting, but in actuality it was a purposeful formation to obscure anyone's view of Mike and keep anyone who happened upon them several feet away from Mike. They all chatted, joked, and smiled, but each of them was on high alert. They passed several of Sandbox's residents. Most of those they passed simply smiled or said hello and went about their way. They had almost made it to Mike's house when they ran into Bobby.

"Well, look at this ragtag group," Bobby said warmly. "Who is that in the middle there? Is that Mike?"

Hobo stepped closer to Bobby. “Sure is. He’s exhausted. We were just walking him home so he can get some rest. In fact, I think we’re all ready to turn in.”

Gray yawned. “Yep, there’s a pillow calling my name.”

Bobby was confused. “Why didn’t anyone see Mike earlier?”

JC chuckled. “You know how quiet Mike can be when he has something on his mind. He was probably just deep in thought and slipped off before anyone noticed.”

The answer seemed to satisfy Bobby, but then he addressed his next question to Mike directly. “It’s great to see you, Mike. Are you hungry?”

“God, I hope he isn’t,” Jordan muttered under his breath.

Gracie, being the only one who heard him, instantly shot him a look that clearly conveyed he should shut up.

“If you’re hungry Mike, I can grab you some stew and bring it over,” Bobby offered.

“Oh, he’s fine. The professor and I took everyone some stew and drinks earlier,” explained Hobo.

“I see,” Bobby replied. He then leaned in closer to Hobo and lowered his voice. “He doesn’t sound very well. Is he sick? Does he need any medicine?”

Capp quickly handled those questions. “I’ve got to be honest with you, he isn’t well. See, I had a couple of cases of beer with me when we arrived. Looted them from a truck stop. I was saving them for a special occasion. What more of a special occasion than arriving here and JC and Mike finally being home? So, we celebrated a little. Mike may have been just a little overserved, if ya know what I mean."

Bobby's face brightened. "I absolutely know what you mean. He was always kind of a lightweight." He turned his attention back to Mike. "Get some rest, my friend, and if you need anything for that hangover in the morning come see me." With that, he bid them all a good night and continued on his way.

"It's alarming how believable you are when you lie," Hobo informed Capp. "Awesome job!"

The next morning Gray awoke in Hobo's guest bedroom. The sunlight flowed in through the sheer curtains, and he could hear birds singing outside. Tooter was still sound asleep next to him on the bed. He decided to let him sleep. After he'd gotten dressed, he followed the smell of food cooking in the kitchen.

"Good morning," Hobo greeted him as he set a plate of pancakes in the middle of the kitchen table. "Please, sit. Just pancakes and eggs this morning, we're running low on meat around here, but I made plenty, and I do have coffee and juice. Which do you prefer?"

Gray smiled at the sight of the food on the table and sat down. "It looks amazing, and coffee sounds incredible."

"Comin' right up."

The two men enjoyed a nice conversation over their breakfast. They discussed their lives both before and after R-Bug, their families, and Sandbox among other things. Gray found he quite liked his host and thought him to be highly intelligent. He could see why JC thought so highly of him.

"Time for dessert," Hobo stated once his plate was empty.

"Dessert after breakfast?" Gray was puzzled. It was the first time he'd ever heard of such a thing. He thought it might be a practice particular to Hobo's family. After all, his own family had some practices and traditions some might view as odd. “Can’t say I’ve ever had dessert with breakfast. I’m stuffed, but I’m down with a little something sweet.”

Hobo snickered. “Not sure if this is exactly what you had in mind, but they are called Hobo Specials,” He produced an expertly rolled “special” cigarette. “Care to partake? Some of my finest work. I make Hobo Cookies too. I suppose those could be considered an actual dessert.”

Gray was caught off guard by Hobo’s offer. He hadn’t been a complete angel during his lifetime by any means, he’d even enjoyed more than one of those “special” cigarettes in the past, but it had been many years ago. He’d had several friends who’d been devoted smokers, but it had always been something he could take or leave. “I appreciate the offer, but it’s been eons since I smoked. Might make me loopy after all this time, and I really want to be clearheaded while we work on getting this whole Mike situation rolling today, but you go ahead.”

Hobo lit the cigarette, inhaling deeply. “Guess I’ll have to smoke your part and mine.” Exhaling he leaned back in his chair and sighed. “Yep, a Hobo Special is the perfect dessert.”

“Other than Mike, what’s the plan for the day?”

“I think JC and Capp are on dayshift Mike duty today, and Jorgen is busy getting things set up in the lab and deciding what test would be appropriate to run on Mike. So, I thought we could get you into a home of your own and figure out a living arrangement for Jordan too.”

Gray hesitated before replying. “Jordan can just stay with me if he wants to. I like the kid, and Tooter seems to like him a lot too.”

"Of course. If that's what you and Jordan want, that's totally up to you. I think we should find something for him to do in Sandbox too. Something to help him feel like he is contributing and being productive. It would be a help to the community, and it seems to me feeling productive helps people keep going, helps keep their sanity."

"I can see that. I would like to add another activity to the list for today too. You said you're low on meats right now?"

"We are." Hobo took another hit from his Hobo Special. "There was a point when we had some pigs, cows, and chickens. When we ran low some of us would go round up more, but it got harder and harder to find more. We had to venture further and further out. I'm sure you know that wasn't the safest or most ideal thing to do. On the last run we decided we would keep any animals we found for breeding. Thought we should replenish the population before we slaughter more. Admittedly, the extra space and food required to keep them is a little bit of a strain, but we're managing."

"While we wait for the farm animal population to replenish, how's the deer and squirrel population around here?"

"We've seen a few."

"The land around Sandbox is pretty overgrown. Deer love that, and I'm pretty good with a bow. A bow is quiet, won't draw the afflicted's attention. You guys have any bows here," Gray asked.

"Unfortunately, no, but there is a small pawn shop in a town not far from here. Might get lucky there, and if not, that town also has a Danterford's."

Gray smirked. "Danterford's are like cockroaches, they just multiplied and spread everywhere. At this point though,

I suppose we should be grateful they did."

"I'm sorry Mike," Jordan apologized. "I know it's a pretty morning, but we can't open the curtains and risk anyone seeing you yet." He led Mike away from the window in his bedroom and over to a chair.

"I found something for you," Grace told Mike. "It's a movie." She popped a disc into the blu ray player and turned on the television. "Have you seen The Neverending Story? It's so good."

"We used to love that movie as kids," JC announced upon entering the room with his cup of coffee.

Mike sniffed the air in JC's direction.

JC took note of Mike's sniffing. "Don't worry, I have your raw meat sitting out now. It should be up to room temperature in around an hour."

Mike grunted, continuing to sniff the air. He then slowly raised his arm and pointed to the cup in JC's hand.

Jordan was astonished. "You don't think he wants the coffee, do you?"

Grace shook her head in disbelief. "No, of course not. Couldn't be."

"He always loved coffee." JC carefully offered the cup to Mike.

They were shocked when Mike attempted to take the cup with his shaky hand. Coffee splashed out of the cup, running down Mike's hand and dripping onto the rug. JC placed his hand over Mike's, holding it just enough to help steady it but so as not to influence or hinder Mike's movements. Grace raced into the other room and quickly returned with a camera Jorgen had given her to record what was happening. Mike pulled the cup to his lips. He sloppily slurped the warm liquid. Under normal circumstances most would have found it disgusting, but JC, Grace, and Jordan beamed with excitement and pride akin to that of proud parents.

Mike half muttered, "Good."

Suddenly they heard Hobo's voice from the bedroom door. "Holy hell! Maybe that Hobo Special was a little too good."

Capp and Gray stood behind Hobo, peering over his shoulder with wide eyes.

After JC explained what had just transpired, Gray asked Jordan to step outside with him for a private chat.

Jordan inhaled the morning air. "It smells so fresh here and the sky is so pretty. It's almost like things are normal. Almost like the afflicted never happened."

"Inside these walls you could just about forget the world ended."

Jordan nodded. "Definitely could, but the world did end, didn't it? Correction, the world as we knew it ended, but the world itself didn't. What they're doing here is proof of that. What Kickz, Tex, and the others are doing in Florida is proof of that. Maybe this was all just God's way, Mother Nature's way, or whoever's way of wiping the slate clean to give us a fresh start. Maybe it was all meant to give us a chance to learn from our mistakes and not make them again. There's just one thing I can't figure out."

"What's that," Gray asked softly.

"Why us? Why you? Why me? Why any of us who are still here? Why were we allowed to live?"

Gray pondered the question for a moment. "To be truthful, I don't know if there is an answer to that. I suppose I could say some higher being picked us for a reason. Possibly that being thought we each had some sort of unfinished business to rectify. Maybe that being saw something in us that made us worthy. Just maybe it's nothing more than luck. The fact is we will probably never know why for certain. The one thing we do know for certain is we are still here which means we have a responsibility to carry on, do the best we can to rebuild, and keep alive the memories of those who aren't still here. That's how we honor them."

"I suppose," was Jordan's flat response.

It was clear to Gray that something was weighing heavily on young Jordan's mind. He knew it could be just the state of the world and the new normal of their lives in general, but he suspected it was more than that. He considered trying to coax it out of him but felt it would be best to let him unburden himself of whatever was troubling him in his own time. "I have a question for you now. Hobo and I are about to go look at places for me to call home here in Sandbox, and I was wondering if you'd want to be my roommate. I like having someone around, and I'm sure Tooter would appreciate it too."

"I think I'll take you up on that. Might be nice to have a home along with somewhat of a family."

Gray scowled at the young man. "What's that mean?

Boy, after all we've been through together, there is no somewhat to it! We are family!"

Jordan remained silent but grinned sheepishly.

They heard the front door open and turned to see Hobo stepping out. "Gents, JC gave me a list of some supplies he needs when we go into town, but first I'd like to show you a couple of homes so we can get you settled in."

Jordan was visibly confused. "We're going to a town?"

"Me and Hobo are," Gray corrected. "We're going to get some hunting gear."

"We're also going to need to run by the pharmacy and the hospital," Hobo interjected. "That's where we'll need to go to get some of the supplies JC requested."

"I want to go," Jordan informed them.

Gray was uncomfortable with the idea of Jordan accompanying them. He knew Jordan was a healthy young man and not a child, but something about his demeanor caused Gray to feel fiercely protective of him. Despite that, he tried to put himself in Jordan's shoes. He knew when he was Jordan's age he wanted to be treated as a man and would have been furious if anyone had treated him in any way that implied he was so incompetent he needed to be protected. "I suppose we could use the extra hands and an extra pair of eyes," he relented.

Gray, Jordan, and Hobo stopped by Hobo's house to pick up Tooter before heading off to look at houses. Hobo instructed them to delay making a final decision until after he'd shown them all the options available to them. The first option he showed them was a charming, two-bedroom house not far from the lab. It was in keeping with Sandbox's medieval theme with some modern amenities and a small yard with a few flower beds. The second option was a three-bedroom duplex that boasted a small but lovely courtyard with a few fruit trees. The third option was a three-bedroom cottage located near the back perimeter wall and across the street from the school. They had just stopped in front of the house when Tooter suddenly sprinted over to the school. He ran straight to Maria who was sitting off to herself while other children played on the playground. Without hesitation, the small dog jumped right onto her lap and proceeded to give her a big lick on the cheek. The little girl's face instantly lit up as a wide smile spread across it.

Gray watched the scene unfold; glad Tooter could bring some joy to the child. "Maria, would you mind keeping Tooter company while we look at this house? I'll come over to get him as soon as we're done."

Marie never uttered a word. She only nodded emphatically while giggling and petting Tooter.

The three men went into the house to have a look around. Just as with the others, the house was very much in keeping with the medieval style with modern conveniences cleverly made to blend in, but it had a cozier feel about it than the others. The focal point of the living room was a stone fireplace with dark stained built-in bookcases on each side of it. Every bedroom featured a window seat with identical built-in bookcases. Warm-rich hardwood floors throughout the house completed the welcoming feel of the home.

"I realize it is sparsely furnished," Hobo

acknowledged, "but we do have a warehouse we've been stocking with various furnishings you can pick from. Of course, you can always scavenge things more to your liking as well. The house does have a small garden plot and a shed out back. As nice as this place is, it does have a drawback."

"What's that," Gray asked.

Hobo motioned to the kitchen window at the back of the house. "One of the watchtowers is right outside that window. There is a lot of coming and going between shifts, noise, and talking. Probably why nobody has picked this place yet."

"Hell, I can sleep through pretty much anything," Gray laughed. "Wouldn't bother me a bit."

Jordan looked through the window at the tower. "I'm completely fine with that tower being there because I intend to take as many of those shifts as I can get."

Gray turned to the young man. "This is home then? It is just us and Tooter. Think we should pass on this one just in case a larger family shows up?"

Jordan shrugged but never took his eyes off the tower. "Hobo said nobody has wanted it because of the noise, right? Plus, I'm not sure why, but something is telling me that extra bedroom will eventually come in handy."

"He's right. Nobody wanted it because of the tower. An added benefit would be a sitter for Tooter whenever you need one because Maria and Alice live just two houses down across the street. Something tells me Maria wouldn't mind having Tooter as a neighbor."

Jordan finally turned from the window to face Gray. "Does that settle it?"

Gray threw his hands up in surrender. "Okay, I guess

we're home. I really liked this place anyway."

Hobo handed him a set of keys. "Welcome home."

After collecting Tooter from Maria, they dropped him off at Mike's for JC and Grace to keep an eye on while they made a run to town. They took the old Ford truck Gray and Jordan had arrived at Sandbox in. Gray drove, Hobo acted as a human GPS from the passenger's seat, and Jordan rode in the truck bed. Occasionally they passed an afflicted wandering on the road, but they were surprised there wasn't more. That changed once they reached the main street in the little town. Gray brought the truck to a slow rolling stop a few feet away from the end of Main Street. An afflicted meandered out of some nearby bushes. Jordan calmly watched it reach for his arm that was resting on the side of the truck bed. Once its half-rotten fingertips brushed his arm, he quietly sunk the blade of his knife deep into its eye. When he withdrew it the afflicted slid down the side of the truck, landing in a crumbled heap next to the truck's back tire.

Gray stuck his head out the window. "You good," he asked in a whisper.

Jordan gave a nod as he pulled a rag from his pocket to wipe the dark blood from his knife blade. "All good."

Hobo looked ahead of them. Dozens of afflicted were stumbling along the street and sidewalks. "We cleared this street weeks ago. We had come here on a run, realized how many there were, and cleared the street, the pharmacy, and the grocery store. We secured those buildings with the intention of coming back to clear and secure the rest of the buildings later, but we haven't gotten back around to it. Even so, it doesn't make sense there would be his many after just a few weeks. Are they migrating or something?"

Gray shrugged. "Maye wherever they were ran out of a food source so, they're wandering around in search of food. Maybe some part of them still associates this town with activity, an instinct pulling them here."

Hobo was completely deflated. "That would add up, especially if any part of them is like Mike. I pray they are nothing like him. If they are, then we didn't just put down the dead when we cleared this town, we killed living people."

"You can't look at it that way," Gray firmly stated. "Looking at it that way will get you killed. We aren't even sure what Mike is. The only thing we do know at this point is that he is different from the others, I don't know if he's some sort of evolution, mutation, or a fluke, but you can bet your bottom dollar any of the ones on this street will kill you. They won't just kill you; they will tear you apart. Do you understand that? You can't hesitate with them for any reason. It's basic survival, us or them. You just chose to survive. You chose to live. There is nothing wrong with that!"

"I'll try to keep that in mind, but I won't lie, after Mike, I don't think I will ever be able to look at them the same again." He shifted nervously in his seat. "Anyway, how are we going to handle our current situation?"

"Think we could park on a side street and walk to the pharmacy without attracting too much attention?"

"Actually, the pharmacy and the pawn shop are right next to each other. There's a back alley right around the corner from them, but I think the truck will draw more attention than if we went on foot from here."

"Good point. I've got some duffle bags behind the seat we can take with us to fill. Where is the hospital and Danterford's? We need to plan this out before we make any move."

Hobo pointed to the other end of Main Street. "They're about three miles that way. Not much around them, but they are across the road from each other."

"Alright then, we leave the truck here, hit the pharmacy and pawn shop, make our way back here, and take the truck to the hospital. We'll make a few passes around the hospital to scout the area out before we stop though."

"After we see what we find in the way of weapons and ammo we should bring some people from Sandbox back with us to clear and secure this town properly."

"Secure it for what," Gray asked.

Hobo shook his head. "Before you guys even came here, I wondered how many survivors were out there and started thinking along the lines of starting to rebuild. I always thought this little town was a good candidate to be part of the rebuilding or at the very least be a good outpost. Since you got here and talked about rebuilding and the settlement in Florida, I've been thinking about it again."

Gray looked at the town before them. If he ignored the afflicted scattered about, he could picture the town as it had once been. It wasn't hard to see it had been charming. "You might be right about this place, but we can't do anything until we complete the task at hand."

The knock at Mike's front door startled JC who was in the kitchen getting an early start on preparing lunch. Laying his knife on the counter, he listened intently. He was desperately hoping the knock had been a figment of his imagination. Another knock dashed his hopes. He slowly crept toward the door, muttering to himself. "Who the hell could that be? The last thing we need is people snooping around here."

He stopped at the door, again listening, and hoping he'd only been hearing things. Again, his hopes were dashed by another knock at the door. With a heavy sigh he opened the door. On the other side stood Alice, the kindly woman who'd taken in little Maria.

Alice greeted him with a bright smile. "Hello. Are you Mike?"

"No, I'm his cousin. May I ask who you might be?"

"Oh, you must be JC!" She extended her hand to JC who pretended to not notice. Alice sheepishly retracted her hand. "Uh, I'm Alice. I've heard all about you and Mike and the story of how the two of you built Sandbox. I came to Sandbox after... Well, after the world changed. Since I never got to meet you before I thought I should come by to introduce myself."

"You're correct, I am JC. Mike isn't here right now. He went with Hobo and a couple of others to obtain supplies. I'll happily let him know you stopped by. Unfortunately, I am very busy at the moment. While it was very nice to meet you, I really must get back to my work. We'll talk again sometime. Bye-bye now."

Alice started to say something, but JC abruptly shut the door before she could. “They said he was a little different, but wow! Just wow,” she mumbled.

Gray, Hobo, and Jordan moved swiftly and silently down the side streets and alleys as they made their way to the pharmacy. Most of the afflicted were on Main Street, but they did run into a straggler here and there. They dispatched them with their knives to remain as stealthy as possible. It didn’t take long for them to arrive at the back of the pharmacy where Hobo produced a screwdriver from his pocket and set about removing the screws that held a sheet of plywood over the back door.

“Y’all did that before,” Jordan asked.

“Yep. We used a drill to put it on, but I couldn’t find it this morning. Suppose it might be a good thing now. The sound of the drill would most-certainly bring the afflicted down on us.”

The back door opened into a storage room. Gray and Jordan immediately began searching the shelves and boxes in that room. Hobo went to the front of the building to gather medications, but within seconds he was calling out to his companions. Gray and Jordan rushed to him with their knives drawn. When they saw no signs of danger they were perplexed.

“What happened,” Gray asked.

Hobo motioned them over to the double front doors. “We secured these doors and the windows last time we were here. Now the plywood is missing from one of the doors, and it looks like someone has been rummaging around in here.”

Jordan tensed. “Afflicted didn’t do that. Who could it have been?”

Hobo looked out the window on the uncovered door. “My bet would be whoever did that.”

Just outside the door they saw a sight that both shocked and frightened them. There was an afflicted tied to the awning support outside the pharmacy. In fact, there were several afflicted tethered in multiple locations up and down Main Street.

“We’re not alone here,” Gray whispered.

The trio retreated to the storeroom to discuss how they should proceed. Jordan had a plan to discover whether or not the culprits were still in town. He’d walk out the front door and travel down Main Street in full view of anyone who might be watching. He’d do so in a manner that made it appear he was simply looting and destroying afflicted along the way, giving no indications he suspected anyone else was around. He hypothesized whoever had tied the afflicted had done it in an effort to keep people out and therefore wouldn’t be far away and certainly wouldn’t take kindly to someone looting.

“You two find somewhere out of sight to watch and cover me. They will come out to stop me, and when they do, we’ll jump them.”

Gray shook his head. “No, absolutely not. I don’t like this, I’ll go.”

Jordan and Gray started to argue, but Hobo cut them off.” Guys, listen! There’s a maintenance ladder to the roof right outside the back door. Don’t let me get dead, boys!”

Before they had a chance to realize what was happening, he gave them a wink, dashed to the front of the store, and went right out the front door.

Gray and Jordan were stunned.

"What the hell was that," Jordan exclaimed.

"Not sure, but we'd better get on that roof!"

They scrambled up the ladder and found the best vantage point to watch Hobo from. Hobo casually strolled down Main Street. He put down afflicted, peeked in windows, and jiggled doorknobs. Naturally, he gained the attention of all the afflicted, including those that weren't tethered. Luckily, they were slow allowing him to dodge them with a fair amount of ease.

Gray's eyes stayed focus on Hobo while Jordan scanned the town for any signs of movement by anything other than afflicted. He was about to give up when he noticed movement in the second story window of a building a few doors down across the street. He angled his head and squinted to get a better look. There was a small flash as if the sunlight was reflecting off something in the window, but not the window itself. He watched for a moment more and saw what was unmistakably movement in that window.

He nudged Gray's arm. "Over there."

Gray followed his gaze and saw the movement in the window. "Let's go."

Weaving in and out of alleys and ducking behind stores, Gray and Jordan attempted to make their way to the building without being seen. At the same time, they were trying to keep an eye on Hobo as best they could. When they couldn't see him, they could at least hear him as he had unexpectedly started to whistle a happy tune while he dispatched afflicted. Upon reaching the back door of their target building they felt confident they'd not been seen since they hadn't been confronted by anyone. They were delighted to find the door was unlocked and unobstructed. Gray positioned himself in front of the door, ready to deal with anything that might come through it. He steadied himself then motioned for Jordan to open the door. With one swift motion Jordan flung it open. Nothing awaited them on the other side.

The men made their way up the stairs where they came to a landing and a short hallway with two doors. One door was to their right and one was at the very end of the hall. They cautiously approached the door to their right. Once again, Gray positioned himself in front of the door, and Jordan opened it. Beyond the door was a small bathroom with no indications of anything living or dead within it. The men remained alert as they moved on to the door at the end of the hall where they repeated the same procedure. This time they didn't find an empty bathroom. Instead, they found a small apartment occupied by two living people, a young man and a young woman. Both were obviously terrified. The pair was backed into the far corner of the room. The man held a baseball bat at the ready. His female companion brandished a large butcher knife. Gray and Jordan raised their pistols.

"Who are you," Jordan barked.

"Just turn around and leave," the man shouted. "We don't want any trouble!"

"You can avoid trouble by answering the question,"

Gray snapped. "And while you're at it, you can explain why those afflicted are tied up out there."

"Those what," the confused woman asked.

Jordan's answer was very blunt. "The dead."

"They're protection," the man informed them. "Protection from your people."

Gray didn't understand. "Our people?"

The question seemed to throw the young man off. His facial expression softened for a moment. "You're not with the people at the asylum?"

Gray and Jordan answered his question with blank stares and shakes of their heads.

The woman lowered her knife. "I believe them, babe," she told the man before turning her attention back to Gray and Jordan. "I'm Trina. This is my boyfriend, Paytan. I do believe you, but make no mistake, you so much as twitch wrong, and I will disembowel you."

Suddenly a scream pierced the air.

Jordan's eyes grew wide with alarm. "Crap! Hobo!"

Jordan bolted from the room with Gray right on his heels. Trina and Paytan followed closely behind them. Outside they found Hobo with his back against the front of a store. He was wrestling with an afflicted as several more were closing in on him. The small group rushed in to help, including Trina and Paytan. While the four of them worked on eliminating the afflicted moving toward him, Hobo managed to push the rather large afflicted man he was struggling with off of him enough to raise his knife and plunge it deep into the creature's ear. The group managed to clear the closest of the encroaching afflicted without anyone being injured, but more were coming from both ends of the street.

"There's more than there was when we first got here," Hobo observed as he tried to catch his breath.

"They're probably coming out of the woods around the town," Gray told him.

"Possibly," Payton agreed, "or they were brought here and turned loose. Let's get back up to the apartment."

Paytan barricaded the apartment door with a dresser. "If they really want in that won't stop them, but it may buy us a little time."

"Who are they," Hobo asked. "For that matter, who are you?" He turned to Gray. "Who is that?"

Gray proceeded to introduce Hobo to the young couple. "Now that we're all acquainted, Paytan and Trina mind explaining what the hell is going on here?"

Paytan took a deep breath. "We used to be with a group of survivors. There were only eleven of us. We got along well and took care of each other. We had a camp set up in the woods near an old asylum not all that far from here. Before that camp we'd all had to move several times, but it went quite well for several weeks at that location until more and more of the dead began to show up. Myself and some of the other men in the group decided maybe the asylum would be a safer place and went to scout it out. We had it in our heads the worst we'd find would be some dead to clear out and maybe some repairs to be done but nothing we couldn't handle. We couldn't have been more wrong.

What we found was another group, a much larger group and we were thrilled. We assumed they would be just as happy as we were to find other survivors. We thought they'd work with us and be decent people. After all there were more dead than living walking around so, it only made sense the living would stick together. The first couple of people we came across at the asylum kinda gave us a strange vibe, but they were nice enough. They gave us a tour of the place. They had a nice kitchen setup, well water, crops growing, and clean beds to sleep in. Not sleeping bags or a pile of leaves with a dirty blanket but real, clean beds! Best of all, they had the asylum walls around the entire property. Walls that used to keep the mentally ill in now kept the dead out." His voice trailed off as his mind took him back to that place.

Gray shrugged. "I don't get it. Sounds like a pretty great place to find in an apocalypse. How'd you end up here, and where is the rest of your group?"

Trina walked over to the window. "One of them is right down there." She pointed to the afflicted Hobo had wrestled with moments earlier. "His name was Shane, and he was a good man."

Hearing Trina say the man's name brought Paytan back to the present. "He was one of the men who went with me to the asylum that day. That place did seem like the answer to our prayers. They told us they regularly took in people and would be happy to have us, but we had to get approval from their leader, a man named Norris. He appeared to be every bit as nice as the others, but something about him felt off. Actually, the man made the hair on the back of my neck stand up. I thought it was just me though. I thought I was overthinking things and being paranoid, but when we got back to our camp to discuss it with the others a couple of the guys said they'd gotten the same feeling. Poor Shane out there was one of them."

Trina picked up the story from there. "When they came back and told us about everything they'd seen we were so excited. Despite some of them voicing their concerns, all we could think about was the safety it offered from the dead. The thought of sleeping in real beds was tantalizing too. We'd been moving around so much we just wanted somewhere to be able to stay awhile. We should have taken their uneasy feelings as a sign. Sure, the first few weeks with Norris and his people were wonderful. They did expect us to earn our keep, but that seemed reasonable to us. We helped with farming, washing clothes, cleaning, guard duties, and supply runs. Sometimes the workdays were long, but again, we saw it as a fair trade for safety, shelter, and food in our stomachs.

One day I was on wash duty with five other women. It was a nice day, they were nice women, and we were having pleasant conversations and a few laughs. We'd been at it around two hours when one of Norris's men came in. He told RaeAnn that Norris wanted to see her. RaeAnn went pale, and the whole demeanor of all the other women changed. They got awfully quiet and just stared at the clothes they were washing. I could tell they were trying to avoid looking at the man or RaeAnn. RaeAnn ducked her head and left with him. I lost track of how long she was gone but it was quite a while, and when she did come back, she looked like she'd been crying and had a busted lip. I asked her what happened and if she was okay. She just turned away from me. One of the other women gave me a stern look and told me RaeAnn would be fine. The tone of her voice made it clear that was the end of the discussion."

"Trina told me about it later that night," Paytan said with a heavy sigh. "It was absolutely a red flag, but I dismissed it. I was so desperate to make things at the asylum work I convinced myself to ignore my own instincts. I tried to convince myself and Trina that she was reading too much into the situation with RaeAnne, but deep down, I knew what had been done to her. I'm ashamed of myself for turning a blind eye. Roughly a week later I wouldn't be able to turn a blind eye anymore." He paused, seemingly struggling to find the courage to continue.

"Go on," Hobo urged. "It's okay."

Paytan took a shaky breath. "Norris had a group that always went out on what he called special runs. Every member of the group was handpicked by Norris, and sometimes they were gone for days on these special runs, and they always came back with multiple truckloads of supplies. We're talking weapons, ammo, food, and medical supplies. All of it was stuff that was becoming harder and harder to find yet, they never failed to find it. We assumed they were able to find it because they must have been traveling a good distance away to find areas and towns that hadn't already been picked clean. They even brought a baby boy back one time. Norris had certain people he was very close to. I guess you could say they were his inner circle. The baby was given to a couple from that circle to raise. When people questioned some members of the group about where they found the baby, they claimed it was in a car on the side of the road. Supposedly, its parents were dead, torn apart by the dead. My issue with that story was the baby looked too healthy. He had no signs of malnutrition, dehydration, or anything. They would have had to have found him nearly immediately after his parents were killed. What are the odds of that? It just didn't sit right with me, but I chalked it up to some sort of divine intervention.

One day, about a week after the incident with Rae-Ann, I talked Norris into allowing me to put together a hunting party because we were running low on meat. We were given permission to take a few rifles and ammo, some knives, and some camping gear. The plan was to stay out for a week, hunting in a different area every couple of days. Our first few days out were okay. We got a couple of bucks and a few squirrels but nothing to brag about. We had a lot of people to feed and wanted to not only get enough meat for use immediately but also get a start on stocking up for the winter. A couple of bucks weren't going to cut it. We decided to take a chance on an area we hadn't originally planned on going to. When we got there, we discovered there was a small community there. It was just a handful of houses and a small store, but it was obvious survivors were there. We could see they'd started putting up a chain link fence among other things. We were going to ask if they knew of the best area to camp and hunt, but just as we were about to step out of the edge of the woods near the store, we heard vehicles approaching. We ducked down and watched as Norris and his special runs group got out of trucks with their guns drawn. Several folks from the little community met them in the street, but we could see others peering out of windows, including kids. I remember thinking they looked absolutely terrified and wondering why. One of the community's men stepped up to meet Norris. Norris's men kept their weapons drawn. There was probably twice as many of his men than there were people in the community, each of them armed while only a couple of the community members were armed.

I heard Norris ask the man if they were packed and ready to go. The man stuttered and stumbled on his words before he finally managed to tell Norris that he and his people appreciated the offer but were going to respectfully decline. He told him they wanted to stay there and make a go of what they'd started. Norris smiled and said he understood, but then he reminded the man he'd told him before either people were with him or they were against him. He said declining meant they were against him, and he simply couldn't have that. The man tried to tell Norris his community had nothing against Norris and wasn't a threat to Norris or the asylum, but Norris just turned his back to him and gave a nod to his second-in-command. With that nod, Norris's men opened fire on everyone in the street then went ahead to hunt down everyone hiding in the houses. No mercy was shown to anyone, not even the kids. As one final insult to all of them, they purposely killed them without damaging their brains and left them to turn."

"What did you and the other hunters do about it," Gray asked, his tone very accusatory.

The pitch in Paytan's voice rose. "What could we do? We were outnumbered! All we could do was watch in horror as they executed those people and then rummaged through the houses and the store. They took everything of any value. That's when it dawned on us why they were always gone for days on their special runs and how they always came back with such good hauls. While they were loading the trucks some of the people they'd just murdered turned. Instead of putting them down they used shields and poles to hold them back, finished loading, and left.

We realized we were living with people truly worse than the dead. The monsters weren't outside the asylum walls, they were inside them. Shane was one of the men in the hunting party. He insisted we should go back to the asylum, gather our people, and get the hell out of Dodge. Part of me agreed with him, but I kept thinking about Rae-Ann. If we ran away, we'd be leaving people like her at their mercy."

Paytan explained he and his hunting party weren't sure what they could ultimately do to deal with Norris, but they were certain they had to go back. Knowing Norris would be suspicious if they'd returned without plenty of meat, they decided to split into two groups to cover more ground and bag more quarry in a shorter amount of time so they could return to the asylum as quickly as possible. They ended up with a fairly decent haul consisting of nine deer, twelve wild turkeys, and a couple dozen squirrels. With their bounty in hand, they started out on their journey back to the asylum. Along the way, they had lengthy discussions about the best way to handle the situation with Norris. Eventually a plan and a backup plan were decided on.

The first part of the plan was to gain the trust of as many of the asylum dwellers as possible. They hoped they could endear themselves to the people enough to gain their trust quietly and quickly. Once they had their confidence, they would enlist their cooperation to expose and overthrow Norris. In the event that plan wasn't working in a timely manner the backup plan would come into play. That plan was very simple, just one of them would gain only one person's trust, Norris's. After gaining his trust that person would get him alone and kill him. They'd felt certain his inner circle saw what a monster he was and would be relieved to be rid of him, but if any of them weren't they'd meet the same fate as Norris.

The scenario didn't make sense to Jordan. "Plan B would have been plan A if it was me. It just makes more sense. Why didn't you see it that way?"

"Honestly, that was our first instinct, but we'd seen what others had been forced to do to earn his trust. We knew the same would have been expected of us, and we didn't think we could hurt innocent people."

Gray walked back to the window and looked down at Main Street. "You're here, your friend, Shane, was walking with the afflicted. Pretty obvious something went wrong. What was it? What happened?"

"RaeAnn happened. Naturally, we weren't going to tell anyone what we'd seen or what we were up to until we determined who could be trusted and who couldn't. For weeks we did our best to make ourselves invaluable to everyone at the asylum and form strong friendships with them. We tried to really become part of them. During those weeks Shane fell for RaeAnn and fell hard. One night, after she'd been summoned by Norris again, Shane told her she wouldn't have to worry about it much longer. Of course, she asked what he meant, and he told her everything. He didn't tell her who was involved in the plot, but he told her everything else. He had no way of knowing what she was willing to do to make what Norris was doing to her stop. She went to Norris with the information the very next day. She thought by doing so it would prove her loyalty to him which would make him see her as something more than a toy to be used and abused. She mistakenly thought he would suddenly respect her and stop violating her."

"I'm guessing it didn't go that way," Hobo gloomily stated.

Paytan looked at him woefully. "Nope. Norris and his men tortured Shane for days to make him give up the names of the others involved, but Shane wouldn't crack. Norris ended up dragging RaeAnn into the room where they were holding Shane. He told Shane if he didn't give him the names RaeAnn would pay the price. To Shane's credit, he tried to hold out, but once Norris and his men started touching RaeAnne he broke. He couldn't stand the thoughts of her being hurt again. Norris supervised while his men did his dirty work and slaughtered everyone Shane named. Trina and I only got away because one of the guys on guard duty took pity on us and allowed us to slip out. We've been running ever since."

Jordan felt horrible for not only Paytan and Trina, but also the people at the asylum. "I always felt lucky Gray and the others found us, but I see now exactly how lucky we were to be found by people like them." He noticed

Paytan's hands were shaking. "Sorry I interrupted. Go on, finish telling us what happened. Was that when you ended up here?"

"We only found this place about a week ago. We were surprised it hadn't been torn apart like most places, and it had very little dead. We rounded up the few dead there were here and tied them up out there like you saw. We hoped they would ward off anybody who might show up or at least be a good warning system. After being here in peace for four days we thought maybe Norris had stopped looking for us. It was wishful thinking. On the fifth day one of Norris's box trucks rolled right up into the middle of Main Street followed by one of his pickups. His men took a dog crate with an old mutt in it out of the pickup and placed it a few feet behind the box truck."

A sarcastic and disgusted snicker escaped Trina. "They knew how I felt about animals, that's why they used that poor dog. They figured it would flush me out which would in turn flush Paytan out. After setting that dog down they opened the back of the box truck, and dozens of dead poured out of it. The dead went straight for the dog, and the men left. I watched the dead getting closer and closer to that dog and couldn't take it. I couldn't let that poor thing be torn apart. Without thinking, I bolted toward it, and Paytan chased after me."

Paytan smiled at her. "Her kindness toward every living thing has always been what I loved about her. I knew nothing was going to keep her from going after that dog, there was no point in trying to stop her. All I could do was try to keep her from getting herself killed. We reached that dog about the same time some of the quicker dead did. We saw right away the crate door was open and couldn't understand why the dog hadn't gotten out. I used my bat and a knife to fend off the dead while Trina tried to coax the dog out, but it wouldn't budge. That's when we saw the blood. Those evil pricks had sliced that animal's hind leg wide open so it couldn't run. I gave the bat and knife to Trina to handle the dead, and I dragged that rather large dog out of the crate. We barely made it back here." He went to stand next to Gray at the window and motioned to the others to join them. "It felt good to save that dog, but while we were doing it, I realized I knew many of the dead they'd released out of that truck, including Shane, RaeAnn, and the guard who'd helped us." He pointed out each individual as he called their name. "I'm sure Norris, knowing we didn't have any real weapons to speak of, assumed we'd get ourselves killed trying to help that dog. I'm also sure, in his warped mind, he saw it fitting to have us torn apart by people we knew. Luckily for us, we weren't as helpless as he thought we were."

Jordan looked around the room. "What happened to the dog?"

Trina brightened. "Come with me." She led them into the small bedroom where the dog was lying on a pallet of blankets in the corner. "Turned out it's a girl. I cleaned and bandaged her leg, but she's still in a lot of pain and can't walk. I think the leg may be infected."

Jordan holstered his pistol and crossed the room to squat next to the injured dog. The dog never raised its head but did release a low growl. "Shh. It's okay, girl. Easy now." He gently pulled back the bandage on her leg and immediately winced. "Yeah, it's definitely infected." He gingerly touched the tip of her nose, narrowly escaping being bitten when she snapped at him. "I'm okay. No harm, no foul. She's in a lot of pain and scared, that's all. I need low dose aspirin, scissors, peroxide, water, antibiotics, fresh bandages, a bottle with a dropper, and either Pedialyte or Gatorade. Not sure if either of those last two can be found anywhere, but they'll go a long way toward helping her."

Trina picked up a pill bottle from a nearby nightstand. "I was going to give her these antibiotics, but I wasn't sure of the dosage since it's human antibiotics." She handed the bottle to Jordan. "I'll run over to the pharmacy to get the rest of what you need. I think I saw some Pedialyte left in the baby aisle over there too."

Jordan inspected the bottle. "Know what, a lot of drugstores fill pet prescriptions. Look for anything like that, it should be clearly labeled. If you can't find any, we'll break these antibiotics down for her. If you can find some turmeric and coconut oil too that'd be great."

Trina nodded. "You got it."

"I'll go with you," Hobo offered.

Capp quietly watched from Mike's bedroom door as JC and Grace played a learning game with Mike. JC held up a picture of a cat while Grace held up a whiteboard with the word cat written on one side and the word apple written on the other side. She asked Mike to point to the word that represented the picture JC was holding. He looked from one word to the other several times before pointing to cat.

“C...c...ca...cat,” he stuttered in a gargled voice.

JC beamed with pride, Grace squealed with excitement, and Capp clapped from the doorway.

“Daddy,” Grace exclaimed, running over to hug him. “I didn’t hear you come in. Did you see what Mike did?”

“I sure did. Awesome job, Mike!”

Mike responded with an excited grunt and one of his twisted grins.

“How did things go, Capp,” JC asked.

Capp took a seat next to him. “We got a good start. To be truthful, I was stunned to see the extent of the tunnels and facilities under Sandbox.”

“Ah, yes, The Underneath. That’s what it has been nicknamed around here.”

Capp was surprised. “You mean everyone knows about it? I’d think something like that would be on a need-to-know basis.”

“It is. You see each building and home in Sandbox has some sort of access to The Underneath because it was designed to be a safe haven in case of any kind of disaster, natural or otherwise, that breeched the village’s walls. There are bunkers down there along with a large cache of food, weapons, and medical supplies. I specifically designed it and stocked it to accommodate the survival of a large number of people for at least five years. So, yes, everyone here knows about The Underneath. However, they do not have access to all of it or even know about all the areas down there for that matter. You are now among the very few who know of all the areas that makeup The Underneath and have access to all of it.”

"You're telling me the labs and such I was just in with Professor Jorgen are part of the secret areas?"

"I am."

Capp shifted in his chair. "I'm honored to have that kind of trust, but I am curious about one thing. You knew Gray and the others were going out to get supplies, why not pull them from the cache?"

"That's a reasonable question that has a two-part answer. First, we always intended for those supplies to be a last resort type of thing. As long as other options were available those supplies were not to be touched. Second, the door those supplies are locked behind requires a code. This code is only known by three..." He paused, searching for the right words. "Um, let's say it is only known by three beings: me, Mike, and GLaDIS. The catch is we each know only part of the code. GLaDIS knows part, I know part, and Mike knows part. It takes all three of us to open that door. It was put in place as a temporary security measure with the intention of replacing it with a better system later, but you know what usually happens when you put things off, you either never complete them or something goes horribly wrong." He looked at Mike. "In this case, both happened."

"That's what comes of you being a procrastinating monster," GLaDIS chimed in.

JC rolled his eyes. "For Pete's sake, GLaDIS! You haven't spoken to me all day, you ignored me when I tried to speak to you, and now you want to start with your sassiness!"

"I'm not being sassy. I am simply speaking the truth."

Capp couldn't suppress an amused chuckle which garnered a stern glare from JC. "Hey, I'm not saying I agree with her! I find the two of you hilarious is all."

"There is nothing hilarious about putting up with the likes of his incompetence," GLaDIS snapped.

JC leaned over to Capp. "You'll want to stay on her good side," he warned in a whisper. "Now," he began in a normal voice, "have Gray, Hobo, and young Jordan returned?"

Capp shrugged. "I haven't seen them."

It was clear Capp's answer concerned JC. "GLaDIS, please, scan the village for Gray, Hobo, and Jordan."

"Scanning now." It took a matter of seconds for her to complete the task. "The three individuals in question are currently not in Sandbox or The Underneath."

Capp was concerned about his friends, but he was also amused by GLaDIS. "Okay, later I want to discuss how freaking cool she is. It's like you've got your very own Penelope Garcia. Is she as cute as Garcia? Answer that later. For now, I think we should be worried about Gray, Hobo, and Jordan. They've been gone a long time.

JC was baffled by Capp's question regarding GLaDIS's cuteness and made a mental note to address it at a later time. "If they're not back within two hours we should put together a search party. As for GLaDIS, she is interesting but certainly not cool."

"Too cool for you," GLaDIS quipped.

Gray, Hobo, and Paytan left Trina to assist Jordan in treating the injured dog while they finished gathering supplies and weapons from the small town. After they were done, they decided to skip the hospital and Danterford's. The decision was made partially because they'd been gone most of the day but mainly because they were concerned some of Norris's men were lurking in the shadows. Jordan, anxious to get the dog back to Professor Jorgen for examination, asked Hobo to help him load it into the back of their old Ford. Once the pooch was positioned safely in the bed of the truck Jordan opted to ride in the back with her, Hobo settled into the passenger seat, and Gray climbed behind the steering wheel.

Paytan and Trina approached Hobo's side of the truck. "It was nice to meet you all," Paytan said. "It was really nice to see there are still good people in the world."

Hobo smiled. "Plenty more good people for you to meet back at Sandbox."

Trina looked at Hobo with bright, hope-filled eyes. "Are you asking us to go with you?"

"I supposc I am, and I can promise you, it will be a totally different experience than the one you had at the asylum."

Jordan laughed. "Oh boy, will it be different!"

Trina turned to Paytan. "What do you think? I know we said we would never trust anyone again, but I truly believe they're good. Anyway, we can't go through life all alone, especially not in this world."

Paytan watched the afflicted aimlessly stumbling about the street. "I know what we said, but I have a good feeling about these guys, and you're right, we can't go through this world alone."

"Then hop on back here with us," Jordan said cheerfully as he rubbed the dog's head. "How do you feel about castles?"

Jordan's question stopped Paytan in his tracks. "Did you

say castles?”

JC and Capp were sitting at Mike's dining room table, sipping coffee, and discussing Mike when GLaDIS interrupted them. "The others just returned. Be advised they are not alone," she warned, immediately putting both men on edge.

"Who is with them," JC inquired.

"I detected an unidentified male, an unidentified female, and a canine."

Capp rose from his seat and called to Grace.

Grace, who was with Mike in the bedroom, happily skipped into the room. "What's up, Dad?"

"I have to take care of something. Will you be okay here with JC and Mike?"

"I'm sorry," JC said as he stood, "but I feel I should go deal with this as well."

"Mike is restrained," Grace told them. "I don't think he would hurt me anyway, but if that's what you're worried about, he is restrained. I will be perfectly fine. Professor Jorgen should be here soon too. I won't be alone with him long."

Capp was very apprehensive. He knew Mike was progressing by leaps and bounds, but he couldn't forget what he technically was, and Grace was his only child. He was fiercely protective of her, but he knew part of protecting her was protecting Sandbox. With that in mind, he reluctantly relented. "Fine, but don't get too close to him. We'll be back as quickly as we can."

The sun was starting to set as they made their way through the streets of Sandbox. Capp and JC noticed many people heading to the drawbridge. Since the virus outbreak started new arrivals to Sandbox were both cause for excitement and a cause for alarm. When they reached the area near the drawbridge, they saw a crowd gathered around the pickup Gray and the others had taken out earlier in the day. They could see Gray, Hobo, and Jordan standing outside the truck talking with a few people in the crowd. Drawing closer to the truck, they saw a young man and woman they didn't know sitting in the back of the truck.

Upon reaching Gray, JC's tone was friendly yet stern. "We were getting worried."

Gray was quick to apologize. "I'm sorry. We ran into some things we didn't expect."

Capp gave a tilt of his head toward Paytan and Trina. "Those things have something to do with those two?"

"Indeed, they did," Hobo answered. "The two of you need to hear their story. I think we all have a lot to discuss."

"There's a hurt dog back there with them," Jordan interjected.

JC peered over the side of the truck. "So there is." He brought his attention back to the other men. "Jordan, there's a cart in the maintenance shop, use it to take the dog down to Mike's. Jorgen should be there by now, and he can help you with the animal. Hobo, select a couple of men to unload and put away the supplies I just saw back there. Gray, grab your new companions there, and follow me and Capp. Hobo, join us after you get men assigned to the supplies. We'll be in the meeting room of the castle."

In the meeting room everyone settled into chairs around the table, with the exception of JC who stood behind a chair at the head of the table. Hobo joined them within a few minutes and took a seat as well. The room was completely silent. JC stared at the newcomers, causing them to wriggle nervously under his gaze.

After several seconds JC broke the silence. "Who are you," he asked flatly.

Hobo spoke up. "This is Tr..."

JC cut him off. "I would like them to answer me." He never took his eyes off Paytan and Trina.

"My name is Paytan, and this is Trina."

JC pulled out the chair in front of him and sat down. "Well, Paytan and Trina, I would very much like for you to tell me everything you told my associates. Do not leave anything out. I want to hear every detail."

He listened quietly for the several minutes it took Paytan and Trina to recount their nightmarish experiences. He did so without displaying any sort of emotion. He never expressed shock, empathy, doubt, or dismay. He only stared with an occasional nod. It was unnerving, even to those in the room who knew him, which was exactly what he wanted. He'd always been of the belief if someone was lying, they would slip and expose the truth if they were a bit unnerved.

When Paytan and Trina finished JC continued to sit in silence for a moment longer before turning his attention to Capp. “We need to fully structure the settlement.”

Capp wasn’t sure what JC meant. “Fully structure?”

“Yes, fully structure. It was something Mike and I always intended for this place. We always envisioned a structured government of sorts as well as an official, trained security team. We started putting the bones of both together but never got around to truly implementing anything.”

Everyone looked at him with curiosity.

“I think I see where you’re going with this,” Capp began, “but just so we’re all clear and on the same page, clarify for us exactly what you’re thinking and how it pertains to the situation at hand with the asylum.”

JC inhaled deeply. “The world and civilization as we know it are gone. Is it horrific? Absolutely. Is it sad? Of course. However, it presents us with a unique set of options. First option, we give up. We simply stop trying and either wait to die or take it a step further and opt out of waiting and living all together.”

Nobody spoke, but they all knew what he was saying. They understood all too well he meant they could wait to die or purposely seek death out.

Hobo shook his head. “Nope. Just nope. What’s the next option?”

“The next option would be focusing solely on keeping our physical bodies alive. We’d hole up here, make sure we eat, and make sure we don’t get eaten. I’m talking purely day to day physical survival. As unappealing as the first option is I personally find this option even less appealing. Truthfully, my feeling is it would be a fate worse than death."

"How so," Gray asked.

"It is nothing more than physical survival. Although it is technically the safest of all the options it gives us nothing to work toward, nothing to have any true feelings about, and nothing to dream about. It is survival, but be assured, it is still a death. It is the death of the very things that make us human, our spirit and intellect."

Capp smiled. "I believe you have a third option in mind, and if it is what I suspect it is you can count me in."

"I do have a third option, and it begins with structure."

Paytan glanced around the room, searching each person's face for any reactions. Unable to discern their thoughts based on their reactions he decided to speak up. "I know I'm new here, and I mean no disrespect at all. Trina and I are very grateful for what you folks have done for us, but we just got done telling you about an asylum not far from here being run by a vicious and evil man, who has equally vicious people doing his bidding. Why are we discussing structure and such when we should be discussing what to do when they find this place? And they will find it, it's only a matter of time."

JC looked at Paytan. "No disrespect taken, but structure and the third option directly relate to the subject of the people at the asylum." He stood and began to pace with his hands clasped behind his back. "The third option would be to look at the world in its current state as a blank canvas to be filled with amazing creations. We could be the ones to fill it. With the help of other survivors and settlements, such as the one

Kickz's group is working on in Florida, we could rebuild this country. It all has to start with structure though. Well, structure and more than basic physical survival. A strong and thriving civilization is built on structure. Structure, when put in place by good people with honorable intent, provides a degree of safety and order for people. While it isn't quite as safe as pure physical survival, the safety and order it does provide keeps chaos at bay. In the absence of chaos spirits and minds have the freedom to grow and flourish."

He stopped pacing, placed his hands on the back of his chair, and looked each person in the eye before continuing. "There is a price to be paid for growth and flourishment though. Leaders and protectors pay that price by being the ones to take risks and to bear the chaos on their shoulders to prevent it from trickling down to the rest of the civilization. They do that by starting with structured rules, a structured chain of command, and structured defense plans. They put those in place with pure hearts and good intent, never with thoughts of controlling the people or self-gain. That is the difference between us and the man at the asylum. I have no doubt everyone in this room has a pure heart and good intent, with the exception of our newcomers." He addressed Payton and Trina. "No offense. We do look forward to getting to know you, but the fact remains, we don't really know you yet."

"We get that," Trina replied very matter-of-factly.

"As I said, for the rest of us, I have no doubt in our hearts and intent. The man at the asylum has put in place the structure, but he did so with a corrupt heart and evil intentions. We need to take a cue from him in the sense of implementing the structure but do it in the right way. If we do that, we can not only handle whatever he may throw our way but also build a better civilization. As a first step, we need to put rules or laws in place. I think the first one should be all newcomers undergo a physical examination and surrender their weapons. They can have them back after they complete a probationary period during which we will evaluate what kinds of hearts and intentions they have." He looked at Paytan and Trina. "Again, no offense."

"None taken. It's a perfectly sensible precaution," Paytan assured him.

"I find everything JC said to be incredibly accurate and exciting." Capp announced. "It would, as he said, ensure a degree of safety, and to be very candid, the thought of living for something more than just trying not to die is exhilarating to me."

"I can get behind that," Hobo proclaimed.

Gray thoughtfully nodded his head. "I'm in."

They were all startled when the door opened, and Jordan stepped into the room.

Gray shot a stern glare at the young man. "What are you doing here? You're supposed to be taking care of the dog."

Jordan walked over to stand at the end of the table. "Jorgen has the dog and says it will mend. Just needs time." He placed his palms on the table and leaned forward. He made sure to look each of them in the eye before he spoke again. He wanted them to see him as a man and to take his words seriously. "I've been standing outside that door listening, and as far as I am concerned, JC is speaking gospel. Lately I've been struggling to see the point of living. JC just helped me see it again. I know I'm young, but I'm not a kid. I want to be part of this."

"What would you like to add to this, young man," JC asked.

Jordan hadn't expected any of them to take him seriously, much less ask for his input. "Okay, uh, I agree with everything you said. I love your vision, but you didn't mention something I think should be an important part of this."

"Go on," JC urged.

"You didn't mention actively seeking out survivors. We would have a better chance at thriving and rebuilding if we seek people out instead of waiting to stumble across them or for them to stumble across us. By doing it that way we would be able to better control who joins us and increase our numbers quicker. We all know there is strength in numbers. Putting all of that aside, it's just the right thing to do. Helping people is just the right thing to do."

Everyone's attention shifted from Jordan to JC who was staring down at the back of his chair, seemingly deep in thought. When he raised his head there was a look of sheer joy on his face and a sparkle in his eyes.

JC pointed to Jordan. "That's what I'm talking about! That's it! He embodies what I meant. He has courage, good intent, and a pure heart. Jordan, tell us what role you would like to play in this."

Jordan took a seat next to Gray. "I want to help protect this place and its people. I'd like to help bring in new people too."

JC sat back down. "I like that, but I've thought for quite some time that you had a more scientific and creative mind than you let on. I thought you might be more inclined to work with someone like the professor."

"I am very interested in that, and at one point that would have been exactly what I wanted. Maybe one day I'll do that, but right now I feel the need to protect this place and find more people stronger than anything else. It's my purpose in life."

Gray wanted to argue with him. He wanted to tell him to stay behind the walls of Sandbox, work with Jorgen, and leave the rest to others. He opened his mouth to say that and more but stopped. He stopped because he knew Jordan was right, he wasn't a kid, and because he could see Jordan had given it a great deal of thought and was very passionate about it. Earlier that day he'd been fearful Jordan was close to breaking down, but in that moment, he saw a fire in him. Gray suspected Jordan's desire to find his mother was a large contributing factor in his decision and still worried about him, but decided maybe it was exactly what Jordan needed, maybe it would be what gave the boy the strength to keep going.

Capp cleared his throat. "I apologize for interrupting, but perhaps we should get our guests situated for the night before we continue this discussion. I'm sure they're hungry and tired. They'd probably like to get something to eat and a hot shower."

Trina perked up. "Did you say hot shower? As in hot, running water?"

Hobo stood up and stretched. "He sure did. Why don't

you come with me? I'll get you set up with a meal, a shower, and temporary accommodation for the night. We'll figure out something more permanent in the morning."

"I know you want to get us out of here so you can talk in private, and I'm cool with that," Paytan said as he and Trina rose from their seats. "You'd be foolish to not be cautious with us until we prove ourselves. I'm thankful to all of you, and I promise we'll do whatever you need us to do."

"We're both thankful," Trina added. "We won't make you regret this. I don't mind telling you tonight will be the first time we've truly slept in weeks. Thank you. Thank all of you."

Capp went with Hobo to get Paytan and Trina situated and assign some men to keep an eye on them. Afterward, they put together a cart of food and drinks to take back to the meeting room. Hobo made a point of adding several notebooks and pens to the cart as well.

"That smells so good," Jordan gushed as they rolled the cart into the meeting room. "I'm starving."

Capp set about unloading food and plates onto the table. "We thought everybody might be a little hungry. We have a lot to discuss, and it'll probably take most of the night. We don't need hunger distracting us."

Hobo went around the table handing out notebooks and pens. "We should take notes. It will help each of us to remember what was discussed and decided, helping ensure we're all on the same page. It'll also serve as reference material later on if needed."

Gray opened his notebook and readied his pen. "Let's get down to business, shall we?"

The first order of business was to figure out who would be head of security. Given Capp's military background, JC thought he was the natural choice. He pointed out that while they had some people who patrolled the walls and manned the watchtowers, they had no real training or organization. He believed Capp would be the perfect person to provide them with both. Capp listened to JC's reasoning before explaining his own position. He let JC know he understood why he had nominated him and appreciated his faith in him, but he didn't feel he was the best man for the job. He was still struggling with his PTSD from his time in the military and worried it could possibly put others in danger. He explained he felt he could be more useful and feel more comfortable working with Professor Jorgen.

"Don't get me wrong, I know I could do what needed to be done in a combat situation if there was no other alternative. I know that because I have improved greatly over the past months, but I thoroughly believe my time would be better spend with Jorgen."

Although disappointed, JC understood and didn't fault him for it. He appreciated Capp's honesty and frankness, but he did ask if he'd be willing to assist in training security. Capp readily agreed and suggested Gray should be head of security and of any teams that would be going out on supply runs or to search for survivors.

"Gray is alert, good with a weapon, and knows how to stay calm under pressure," Capp informed them. "I can teach him some tactics and techniques I learned during my time in service and help him train anyone under his command. He will still have a massive job heading security and teams going outside of Sandbox. For that reason, I believe he needs a second-in-command, and I think that it should be Jordan. He's proven himself to be capable. He's young, healthy, and eager. Judging by what he said earlier, its' a job he would be very passionate about."

"Gray, Jordan, it would mean the two of you would largely be responsible for enforcing the laws inside these walls too," JC advised. "Are you comfortable with that?"

"We are," Gray confirmed. "We're your men." He hoped Jordan picked up on the way he phrased his response.

After that was settled, they went about putting the rest of what they dubbed The Committee in place. Along with lending a helping hand to Gray and Jordan, Capp would also act as Jorgen's lead assistant. He would take on such responsibilities as helping Jorgen put together a bare-bones medical staff with available people until more traditional medical professionals could be found, assisting Jorgen in overseeing the scientific team conducting the research on Mike, and heading up all IT operations for Sandbox. In the midst of all of it, he would also be Jorgen's student, learning as he went. JC worried Capp was undertaking too much, but Capp vowed he could not only handle it but welcomed it.

With those duties delegated, they moved on to Hobo's role. Hobo would oversee the day-to-day operations of Sandbox such as farming, cleaning, and assigning jobs to people. His responsibilities would also include setting up and organizing a pantry and an armory as well as being somewhat of a liaison between The Committee and the people of Sandbox. Hobo was pleased with those duties, particularly his liaison role, because he'd always loved Sandbox and the people who lived there. He cherished his relationships with them and felt in his heart there was nothing they couldn't do or overcome when they worked together.

To most at the table, the natural selection to be head of The Committee and Sandbox's leader was JC. He would oversee everybody and have the final say in all matters. JC didn't agree with them. He made it crystal clear he felt the best man to fill that role was Mike, but in light of Mike's condition, he would accept the role.

"I need all of you though. No one person can do this alone. It is imperative for any leader to have good people they can trust by their side. There is no one I trust more than the people in this room."

"Does that include me," GLaDIS unexpectedly asked. "I am technically in this room. I am technically everywhere."

JC ducked his head, "GLaDIS, have we not discussed eavesdropping more times than I can count?"

"We have discussed that subject matter a total of one hundred thirty-one times. Based on your question, am I to assume you lack the ability to count that high? Perhaps you should attend some classes at the school with the children."

Everyone fought the urge to laugh, but a few snickers managed to escape some of them. JC was the only one who didn't find it amusing. "Despite your snarky, smart-assed attitude, yes, GLaDIS. Yes, I trust you."

"I appreciate that. Will you, because you trust me, take my advice and attend classes? I would think the leader of a civilization should be able to count much higher."

Capp could no longer contain himself. He burst into a thunderous roar of laughter causing a chain reaction with the others. The room filled with the sound of their laughter.

"Damn it," JC exclaimed. "Do not encourage her! She is not funny in the least!"

Capp, who'd laughed so hard his face was red, struggled to catch his breath. "JC, we love you, but she is fricking hilarious! I suppose that could be a compliment to you too."

JC's eyes narrowed, and his tone became indignant. "How so?"

"Well," Capp gasped. "You had the good sense to recruit her, didn't you?"

The response flabbergasted JC. Until that moment, it hadn't occurred to him that they didn't know about GLaDIS, he'd never told them, but it explained what Capp had said earlier. "I didn't recruit her, I created her. I didn't think to tell you that before. She is an AI."

The laughter in the room abruptly stopped. They'd all wondered why they had never seen her and thought her voice and mannerisms were strange, but none of them had made the leap to determining she was artificial intelligence.

After sitting in stunned silence for several seconds, Capp suddenly started to laugh maniacally. "That makes it even better! You created her which means, in some ways, she is part of you. So, not only are you a damned genius, but some part of you is sassy and funny as hell too!"

JC still wasn't sure that was a compliment, but he chose to let the matter go.

Capp then addressed JC's antagonist. "GLaDIS, since I will be working in IT here, I suppose I will be working with you quite a bit, and I am really excited about that, but please, go easier on me than you do JC."

"I am sure we will have limited issues," GLaDIS replied. "You're not a monster like he is, and I assume you are intelligent enough to count higher than he can."

Her statement evoked another round of laughter from everyone.

JC rolled his eyes, "Okay, I believe comedy hour is now drawing to an end, and we should push forward with the business we are here to discuss. Are you agreeable to that, GLaDIS?"

"You may proceed, you monster."

Hobo raised his hand with a little wave to get everyone's attention. "Maybe we should fill each other in on what our initial plans in our new, official roles will be."

JC found that to be an excellent idea. "Alright, Hobo, let's hear from you first. You have the floor."

"A consolidated armory is a great idea, but if we are going to search out more people, we're going to need as many weapons and as much ammo as possible. In fact, I think we should build a facility adjacent to the armory to manufacture ammo. I'm certain, with all the intelligent people we have in Sandbox, somebody already knows how to make at least some forms of ammo, or we can learn. Considering we are going to be searching out more survivors and the situation with the people at the asylum, I feel we should start on that building immediately."

"Me and Jordan can put together a team to go out for weapons, ammo, and building supplies," Gray told him.

"I'd appreciate that," Hobo replied. "I'd like to be on that team. I know some of the best places to look in this area, and while we're out there, I'd like to scout areas for outposts and satellite settlements. Speaking of which, that was the other thing I wanted to bring up. I feel very strongly that outposts and satellite settlements will be important for a variety of reasons."

Gray couldn't agree more. "Absolutely. Suppose something were to happen here at Sandbox, whether it be an attack by the living or by the dead, and there was a need for retreat. Outposts stocked with weapons and supplies could be the difference between life and death."

"They could be the start of more places similar to Sandbox or Kickz's settlement," Capp added. "They could be the start of full-blown communities and towns, which will lead to the rebuilding of at least this country and humanity. There will need to be ways to communicate with each of them. We should start working on that. We could use things like CB radios and such while we work on getting other lines of communication in place."

Gray, who'd been taking many notes, scribbled furiously in his notebook. "CB gear added to the shopping list for the team."

"Do you know what to look for," Capp asked.

Gray smiled. "My dad and cousin were both into CBs. I was raised around both mobile and base stations. I was also into amateur radio too, even licensed."

It was Capp's turn to smile. "One more reason you're a good man to have around."

Jordan decided it was a good time to throw out some ideas he felt especially strong about. "Guys, I know we're going to be training an assigned security team, but with threats from the living and the afflicted, I think everyone aged ten and up should have some self-defense and weapons training."

JC was curious. "Why so young?"

"The kids are the future of humanity, and it's up to us to give them every tool we possibly can to make sure they survive to fulfill that destiny. It's our duty to do that, and of course, we will all do our very best to protect them, but we're living in a very unstable and dangerous world. They need to be prepared in case they find themselves in a situation where none of us can protect them. They need to be taught basic life skills too. I'm talking about things like farming, cooking, and first aid."

"You are wise beyond your years," JC remarked. "I'm glad you're here with us. I would like to add something as far as the children go. It would be wise to have an evacuation route and plan in place. Everyone should know it, but especially the little ones."

Capp perked up. "The Underneath would be perfect for that, and I have an idea, but I need some time to work out the logistics."

"What's The Underneath," Gray asked.

"It's an underground facility beneath Sandbox," Hobo informed him. "Most don't even know it exist."

Capp shifted anxiously in his seat. "I... I'm sorry. I guess I just feel so comfortable with everyone here I just let it slip."

"Nonsense," JC exclaimed with a dismissive wave of his hand. "Every person in this room has proven themselves to be trustworthy. Now that you mention it, each member of this committee should know Sandbox inside, out, and underneath. Hobo, if you don't mind, tomorrow take Gray and Jordan down, and give them all the info about the Underneath, including all codes."

Hobo gave him a nod. "Consider it done."

"This whole conversation has been productive, and at least on my part has given me a new perspective on the future. I feel truly hopeful about the future for the first time because we have some structure and a plan," Capp shared. "Because of that, I hate to break the flow, but we have to tackle the asylum issue because right now they may be the biggest threat to our future. Gray, Hobo, Jordan, you were there with Paytan and Trina, and you saw what they claim those people did. Do you believe them? What are your thoughts on the threat level?"

Jordan didn't hesitate to share his opinion. "I was hoping we would get to this tonight. I do believe Paytan and Trina, and my honest thought is the people at the asylum are a bigger threat than the afflicted. The afflicted, to a degree, have an excuse for what they do and what they are. They aren't doing anything out of malice. On the other hand, the asylum people are making the conscious decision to do the malicious things they are doing and to be what they are. They have the ability to think, reason, and feel, and they still choose to be what they are. They are purposefully cold and evil. Add that to the fact they can strategize, and they instantly become more of a threat than the afflicted. We need to be prepared for that threat. We've all become accustomed to putting down afflicted without hesitation, fear, guilt, or shame. We should accept the fact we may have to start doing the same with humans."

Gray nodded emphatically in agreement. "He took the words right out of my mouth. We need weapons and solid training asap. I suggest we put in place two dedicated teams, each one with specific purposes that are their only focus, instead of one team to handle it all. One team would be a security team for Sandbox. They would enforce the laws and procedures of Sandbox, protect and defend Sandbox, and if something were to go wrong, evacuate and protect the people. The members of that team wouldn't go on runs or anything like that, their sole purpose would be to defend this place and the people within its walls. As for the other team, I suppose you could call it our offensive team. They would be the ones to go on supply runs, but on each of those runs they would also look for survivors and scout locations for new outposts and settlements. They'll also be the team to initiate strikes against threats and enemies when need be, such as with the situation with the asylum."

Capp raised an inquisitive eyebrow. "Are you suggesting we should initiate an attack on the asylum?"

Gray looked him square in the eye. "Yes, I am."

Capp inhaled sharply. "It's risky for certain, but I think

it's the right move. Those people have demonstrated a viciousness within them that won't allow them to do anything short of coming for us in the most violent way possible. They will show up here sooner or later, and it could be at a time when our guard is down. Until then, we'll be living in fear, constantly looking over our shoulders. If we're going to do it though, we'd better make our move soon. I'd bet they're already calculating theirs."

Everyone looked to JC for his reaction, but he was deep in thought, seemingly oblivious to the eyes on him. On the outside he was stoic, but inside he was a tangled mess of thoughts and emotions. He knew they only had three options; abandon Sandbox and flee, wait for the enemy to come to them, or strike first and strike hard. He wouldn't even consider the first. Too much work had gone into Sandbox, and too many people depended on it. Besides, where would they ever find another place like it? It was the perfect setup for day-to-day living, building a future, and scientific advancements.

With abandonment ruled out, he carefully considered the other options. They could very easily spend their time preparing Sandbox and its citizens for an attack on their home turf and otherwise, continue with life as usual. The advantages of that would be remaining behind the safety of their walls and knowing more about Sandbox itself and the terrain around it than their attackers. Capp had already pointed out the disadvantages. They would be living in more fear than they already were, and if the attackers caught them at a vulnerable moment the results could be devastating. JC took that reasoning a step further. He knew when people were overly anxious they were more likely to make mistakes, and in this situation, mistakes would certainly prove to be deadly. Then there was the fact that even if they managed to stave off an attack on Sandbox, possibly even wiping out all attackers, they wouldn't know how many more would be waiting back at the asylum to avenge their friends' deaths.

Taking all of that into consideration, he knew an offensive show of force was the only real option they had. It was the same strategy he had used in games a million times over the years, but this was different. When he led an army into battle in games, he was nervous about losing equipment, gear, or weapons, but he was never scared. He never feared losing the beings he was leading into war; they were pixels after all. They would either respawn or be easily replaced. He didn't fear dying himself because he would simply respawn, often in the safety of his own base. While games had taught him a great deal about strategizing and making tough decisions, they couldn't teach him about true fear, the fear he was feeling in that moment. He desperately feared for the people he would be sending into battle against the asylum group. These were living, breathing humans he considered family and friends. Being made of flesh and bone instead of pixels, there would be no safe or happy respawn for them. The chance some of them would die was high, and those who survived would have emotional and mental repercussions to deal with. None of them would escape unscathed.

JC pushed his fear aside and cleared his throat. "You're right, we need to strike first, but we must be smart about it. We need an idea of the number of people we will possibly be facing and the layout of the asylum and its grounds."

"I'll put together a recon team," Gray offered. "It will be a good chance to evaluate people for possible placement on our offense team. We'll go tomorrow night and get there just before dawn. In the dark, we'll be able to see the areas they have lit up and determine any dark, blind spots they may have. Once the sun comes up, we'll be able to get a better view of the layout, the people, and guard positioning."

Capp was pleased with the plan. "That's smart."

JC thought it was too. "I like it. We should take Paytan with us. He will be very useful."

Capp frowned. "He will be, but what do you mean by us?"

"I mean myself, Gray, and whoever he assigns."

Gray and Capp exchanged concerned glances.

"Excuse my bluntness," Gray said, "but you're not going with us, JC."

Capp leaned forward. "He's right, JC, you're not going. You are the leader here and the heart of Sandbox. That's too important to put at risk. On top of that nobody knows the inner workings of the systems here like you do. That knowledge cannot be put at risk under any circumstances. It's best for you to stay here, focus on Mike, and keep everyone calm. You need to assure them we have everything under control and help them understand and accept the job titles and structure we're putting in place."

"Listen to the man, JC," Hobo urged. "It is the best thing for all concerned."

"I'm glad you see it that way," Gray smiled, "because

you're not going either, Hobo."

Hobo was offended, "Why the hell not? I'm not JC, and I may not be the best at combat, but I can hold my own!"

Gray shook his head in exasperation. "Hold on! Everyone here knows you can handle yourself just fine. We never thought you couldn't. Now, you may not be JC, but you are his right-hand man. You also have knowledge of this place and its people that nobody else has, and these people look to you for reassurance and guidance as much as they do JC."

"I'd say they look to him more than me," JC observed. "He's more of a people person than I am. That's a small part of why I depend on him so much."

"It's settled then. Both JC and Hobo will stay here," Capp declared. "JC can keep in touch with the recon group by radio while Hobo decides who would be the best candidates to be placed on the team to defend Sandbox." He then addressed Hobo directly. "You know these people and they know and trust you. Gather them together, explain what we may be facing. They shouldn't be kept in the dark on this because they need to be prepared. You know their strengths and weaknesses. Pick the ones you think have the qualities and skills to form the best security team possible."

They discussed a few more details then relaxed for a while with snacks and light-hearted conversation about things such as their favorite games, music, and life before the afflicted. It was not only enjoyable, but it also served a purpose. It wasn't verbalized by any of them, but they all knew what it was and understood how important it was. It was giving them a sense of calmness and reminding them of why they were doing what they were doing with Mike and why they were going to do what they were at the asylum. They needed that at the time. They were doing it all to give the good people left in the world a chance to have a life like or better than the one they had before the afflicted and to one day prevent anyone else from facing the horror of becoming one of the afflicted. Each of them understood how lofty those goals were, but they also understood someone had to take on the weight of those goals otherwise humanity was facing almost certain extinction.

Capp looked around the table with affection for the men seated at it. The period of his life when he didn't know them hadn't been that long ago, but he felt like he'd known them for a lifetime. He carried a heavy sense of loss and sadness over the state of the world, but he was grateful that in the midst of it all, he'd found this group of people. "Gentlemen, I just want to say I'm proud to work with each of you. I can't think of anyone else I'd rather fight beside at the end of the world."

As JC listened to the pleasant conversation and pondered all that was about to happen, he was reminded of a quote often misattributed and considered to be a paraphrase but still one of his favorites. "Evil prevails when good men do nothing." With a smile, he looked at the group before him and whispered, "Evil doesn't stand a chance."

The group adjourned for the night, and JC went to relieve young Grace of her duties with Mike. Capp accompanied him so he could take Grace home with him. They were flabbergasted by what they found upon their arrival at Mike's house.

"Grace, what are you doing," Capp snapped.

Grace and Mike were sitting side by side at the kitchen table. Mike was secured quite well to his chair at his waist and legs, but his arms and hands were free, and he and Grace were coloring. The sound of Capp's voice startled them, evoking a horrendous sound, almost a shout mixed with an unnatural groan, from Mike.

Grace was visibly perturbed. "Daddy! You scared us! What are you shouting about?"

Capp rushed over and yanked the girl from her chair and out of Mike's reach. "Why are his hands loose? What were you thinking Where is the professor?"

Grace rolled her eyes. "The professor has only been gone about twenty minutes. He had to go do something with that hurt dog's IV, and I was thinking it would be awfully hard for him to color with his hands tied to a chair. Duh!"

"Dear girl, I'm sure you meant well, but your father is right to be concerned," JC stated gently but firmly. "I love Mike, but you should not be alone with him when he is unrestrained."

Grace looked at Mike who almost seemed hurt. "Keep coloring, Mike. We'll be right back, and I want to see a pretty picture when we get back." She motioned for Capp and JC to follow her into the bedroom where she proceeded to let the men know exactly how cross with them she was. "You know, for two intelligent, good men, you two can be real asshats!"

Capp, shocked by his daughter's anger and cursing, physically took a step back. "Young lady, you're treading on very thin ice! Get control on yourself and apologize."

Grace folded her arms across her chest and raised her chin defiantly. “I will not!”

Capp was completely flustered. “You… you… you… you absolutely will!”

Grace grew more defiant. “Nope.” Capp started to speak, but Grace quickly continued before he could. “You both hurt his feelings, and that makes you asshats! It was uncalled for! You can’t say you want to help him find his humanity again and completely disregard his feelings at the same time. It’s almost like you don’t think he has feelings. A person with no feelings doesn’t have any humanity in them. So, which is it, do you believe he still has humanity in him or not?” This time both men opened their mouths, but the tiny girl silenced them by holding up one hand. “Furthermore, I am not stupid. I knew the risk,” she pulled a knife from the sheath on her belt, “and I was prepared to do what I had to. However, I didn’t need to use this because he was perfectly well behaved. I’d say he showed a lot of progress. He even let me know when he was hungry, and I got him some ham.”

JC’s curiosity was piqued. “What kind of ham? I think the only ham in the fridge is slices of cured ham. Did he actually eat that?”

Grace’s lips curled into a wide grin. “Yes, it was the cured ham, and he ate five slices. At first, he made a face like it tasted bad to him, but I explained learning to eat normal food again was part of how he would get back to being himself, and he kept eating it. He even smiled. I was worried about how the high amount of salt in the ham would affect his body though, what with it being in such a fragile state and most likely dehydrated. I ended up giving him some water."

By that point, Capp had calmed considerably, and his curiosity took over. "What did he do?"

"He drank it. As a matter of fact, he drank a lot of water. He was terribly thirsty."

"Then what happened," Capp pressed.

"We colored, and he is getting much better at it. He only used one color, but he stayed in the lines. Come look."

Grace darted back into the kitchen, followed by Capp and JC. Both men grew nervous again when she walked right up to Mike and reached for the coloring book he was working in, her arm just inches from Mike's mouth. Mike's hand stopped moving, the tip of his crayon still poised above the little dog's ear he'd been filling in. He stared at Grace's arm in front of him.

"Can I show them, please," Grace sweetly asked.

Mike slowly turned his head to look up at her with a smile. He removed his hand from the coloring book and gave her a nod.

"Thank you." Grace picked up the coloring book and gasped when she looked at it.

The smile on Mike's face dissipated when he saw her reaction, and he lowered his head as a puppy might when being scolded.

Grace placed her hand on his shoulder. "Oh, don't feel bad, Mike. I did that because I was surprised by how good you've done. This is even better than the one you colored earlier."

Mike looked back up at her. His smile had returned.

Grace turned to Capp and JC as she flipped a page back in the coloring book. "Look, this is what he did earlier. It was all blue, but it was all inside the lines."

Capp took the book from his daughter and held it in such a way as to allow JC to see it too. They gazed upon a picture of flowers with butterflies fluttering around them. Mike had indeed used only the color blue but had kept the color neatly within the lines. "I'll be damned," Capp muttered.

"You haven't seen anything yet," Grace exclaimed, the excitement in her voice unmistakable. "Turn to the next page!"

Capp did as she instructed, and his and JC's jaws dropped. Before them was a scene of a spotted pup playing with a ball, but it wasn't a blue pup or a blue ball. Instead, the pup was colored brown with black spots, and the ball was red. One of the pup's floppy ears was brown while the other was black like its spots but unfinished. It was obvious it was the ear Mike had been so intently working on. Just as with the previous picture, Mike had colored neatly within the lines. For most people, none of what Mike had done with either picture would be extraordinary, but for someone in his condition, it was nothing short of miraculous, a fact that did not escape Capp nor JC.

JC beamed with pride. "Mike in such a short time, you've made progress in leaps and bounds. This is remarkable."

Mike's smile grew, and his eyes sparkled.

Capp gently placed the coloring book back on the table in front of Mike. "Uh, Mike, that's a fine job you've done. I understand you're a grown man, but your cousin here is right, this is remarkable progress, and I was thinking we could honor it the same way I used to honor Grace's progress."

Upon hearing her father's words, Grace squealed and clapped her hands. "That's a great idea! Finish the puppy's ear, Mike."

Finishing the pup's ear took Mike a few minutes because his movement was stiff and his hand was shaky, but JC noticed it was steadier than it had been previously. Once the ear was finished, Grace carefully tore the page from the book and handed it off to Capp, who made a production of putting it on the refrigerator for display.

"Like I said, I know you're grown, you're not a child, but this is amazing progress, and it deserves to be honored, even if it is in the only small way we can right now."

"It sure does," Grace gleefully exclaimed. "Mike, Daddy used to do that for me all the time. It made me feel so proud, but that wasn't all it did. See, whenever I saw something of mine on the fridge, whether it was while I was getting something to drink or just passing through the kitchen, it reminded me that I'd done something good. No matter if it was a picture I'd colored or if it was a test I'd aced, it reminded me I'd done something good because I'd tried my best, and that made me want to try harder and do more. Every time you see that picture of that puppy, I want you to remember how hard you tried and how well you did. Let that push you to try harder and do more. Will you do that for me?"

Mike nodded his agreement in his abnormal, jerky way.

"Promise," Grace asked.

Capp, JC, and Grace expected another jerky nod, but

they weren't in anyway prepared for what he did next.

Mike suddenly grabbed Grace's hand with a speed none of them thought he was capable of. Wrapping his pinky finger around hers, he stammered, "P...p...pinky...p... pomis."

The following morning, Gray and Jordan were up before most others in Sandbox. They wanted a chance to take a full inventory of weapons and get the entire layout of Sandbox without any interruptions. They mapped out every nook and cranny of the village, making notes along the way of any areas that could possibly be vulnerable to attack. As they inspected the outside of Sandbox's large wall, Jordan put down two afflicted they found clawing at it.

"You know," Jordan began as he wiped the afflicteds' blood from his knife, "if the afflicted were the only worry we had, this place would be a fortress."

Gray continued to look over the notes they'd taken during their inspection. "A fortress as far as typical afflicted go, but maybe not where ones like Mike are concerned."

"Do you think there are more like him?"

Gray looked up from his notes. "I'm not sure, but it stands to reason there might be. That possibility combined with the threat of people like the ones at the asylum are why we have to beef up defenses around here and make sure the people on the other side of this wall know how to defend themselves."

Jordan looked at the two afflicted he'd just put down. "These didn't seem anything like Mike, and they're not wet, so they weren't smart enough to find a way across the moat, and they didn't walk or swim across it. Maybe a tree has fallen across it, and they're just getting lucky when they stumble across it. Stuff like that and the cracks we've found in the wall are the types of things that need to be monitored constantly and squared away immediately when they're found. Maybe we should look at putting together a maintenance team too."

"Jordan, look at the way the afflicted move and walk. What do you think the odds are of them making their way across a downed tree without falling? Personally, I believe those odds are incredibly low, unless they had help."

"The people from the asylum?"

"Possibly. A maintenance team is a good idea, it's needed. Once we have it assembled, any time a member of maintenance is outside the wall they should be escorted by a couple of members of security. As a matter of fact, nobody should ever be outside the wall alone for any reason. As for how these jerks made it across the moat, we have to consider they may have had some help. We need to find where they got across."

They continued their inspection of the wall while simultaneously looking out for any signs of where the two unwelcome visitors might have made their way across the moat, but nothing stood out to them. They were about to give up when Jordan spotted a suspiciously placed brush pile on the other side of the moat. They made their way back to the front of the wall and had GLaDIS lower the drawbridge for them to cross the moat to inspect the brush pile. Both men, with pistols drawn, approached the pile with caution. They were hyperaware of every aspect of their surroundings. Once they reached the pile, Gray kept his gun at the ready while Jordan holstered his and cautiously pulled loose limbs and leaves off the pile. Eventually a rather large log with ropes tossed haphazardly on top of it was revealed.

"Take a look at this."

Gray stepped closer and looked down at the log and ropes. In his mind, they confirmed his suspicion someone had helped the afflicted across the moat. It didn't take long before he saw something that would have removed any doubts had he had any. "Look closer at the ropes."

Jordan did as he was told. Upon closer inspection he saw bits of rotten flesh caught in the rope fibers. "These ropes were tied to afflicted."

"Looks like they led them here with the ropes, put the log across the moat, led the afflicted over, cut them loose, ran back across and pulled the log back. That still leaves us with three pretty pressing questions. Number one, who exactly are they? Number two, why did they do it? Number three, how did they do it without one of the lookouts in the tower seeing them?"

"I think the third one bothers me the most." Jordan pointed to the tower in front of them. "The tower is right there. There is a clear view from it to this spot. Whoever was up there couldn't have missed it! I don't think those afflicted were at the wall yesterday, so it had to have happened last night."

"We need to burn this log and find out who was in that tower last night." The tone of Gray's voice was grim. "We may have a traitor in our midst, and the asylum people may already have someone inside Sandbox."

Gray and Jordan immediately went to JC with their discovery and their suspicions. JC quickly requested Hobo join them. The situation was explained to Hobo, and he was asked if he knew who had been on watch in the tower the night before.

"I believe it was Chester," Hobo answered. "He couldn't possibly have been involved though, he's a good man."

"We're not saying he was involved," JC assured him. "What we are saying is that something went horribly wrong, and we need to find out why."

Hobo wasted no time in tracking down Chester to escort him back to JC, Gray, and Jordan in the meeting room.

JC greeted the man in a light and friendly manner. "Nice to see you, Chester. Come in and have a seat."

Chester took a seat. "It's nice to see all of you."

Chester was a tall, slightly heavyset man in his early sixties. He'd spent much of his adult life as the head of a power plant and married to his high school sweetheart. He had retired only a matter of months before the world ended. Upon retirement, he and his wife sold their home and moved to Sandbox. They'd heard about Sandbox from a friend and thought it sounded like a little piece of Heaven on Earth. They had no way of knowing only three short months later his precious wife would pass away from an undiagnosed heart condition. Chester had been utterly devastated and turned to the bottle for comfort. In the beginning, his drink of choice had been rum, but after the world changed and rum became harder to find, he started settling for whatever he could get his hands on. More than once he'd found himself drunk, sitting on the wall surrounding Sandbox, watching an afflicted stumble through the woods, and wondering if he'd be better off trading places with that poor soul.

Hobo had been the one to figure out Chester had a problem. He sympathized with Chester, but he knew it was a dangerous addiction, especially with the state the world was in. He'd feared Chester's drinking would get Chester or someone else killed. He'd sat Chester down and shared his fears with him. Chester had been horribly embarrassed but had known Hobo was right. Together they'd implemented a plan to help him get sober, and Hobo had been there for him every step of the way.

JC spoke to Chester gently. "Is there anything about last night you'd like to tell us, Chester? Is there anything you need to tell us?"

Chester was visibly confused. "Um, I don't think so. It was a pretty typical night."

Although JC was being gentle and friendly, Gray had a much different approach. "Last night was not a typical night, and you know it," Gray shot back in a stern and accusatory fashion.

Hobo was shocked and a bit angered. "Now wait one minute there, Gray!"

Chester stopped him. "No. No, Hobo. I lied. It wasn't a typical night at all. I did something rather stupid, and I am so sorry."

Hobo's heart sank. "What did you do Chester?"

"It was my night in the far tower. It started out normal enough. I went up there with my thermos full of coffee, my rifle, and a book and got settled in for the night. A couple of hours in I was reading my book when I realized I had the munchies. I decided to run back to my house to grab snacks. Figured it wouldn't hurt because I'd only be gone five minutes at the most. On my way back I saw a bottle sitting on one of the picnic tables near the school. I always try to pick up any garbage I see around the village. Outside these walls are places with trash and debris everywhere, but it doesn't have to be that way in here. Anyway, I went over to get it with the intention of throwing it away, but that's when I saw it was a half-full bottle of whiskey." He turned to face Hobo. "I knew I should pour it out. I kept telling myself to do that. I wanted to do that, but that old craving came back. My hands started to shake, and before I knew it, I was carrying that bottle up into the tower with me. I told myself I would just take a couple sips, just enough to steady my hands, then I'd pour out the rest and throw the bottle into the woods outside the wall. Things didn't happen that way though."

"How did they happen," Jordan softly prodded.

Chester looked defeated. "I drank it all. I drank every last drop and passed out at some point. I woke up about thirty minutes before my replacement was to show up this morning. It was just enough time for me to hide the bottle, drink some coffee, and straighten myself up enough I didn't look like I'd been... Well, like I'd been doing exactly what I did."

"That's it," Hobo asked. "Nothing else happened? You didn't see or hear anything?"

"No. Wait, I thought you'd found out what I'd done and that was why I was here. That isn't it though, is it? What aren't you telling me?"

"Where did you hide the bottle," Gray asked. "Did you throw it in the woods?"

"No. The sun had come up by then. I was afraid someone would see me then. I hid it under a loose board on the tower stairs. It was like the third step from the top."

Hobo rose from his seat abruptly. "I'll be right back." He left the room but returned quickly, the empty whisky bottle in his hand. "Found it right where he said it would be."

With Chester's story verified, Gray's attitude towards him softened. "I was harsh with you, and I apologize. Some things happened last night that put us in the position of needing to be a little skeptical of you until we got your story and confirmed it." Gray went on to tell Chester what they'd found earlier and what they suspected had taken place the night before.

Instead of being relieved by the fact they now knew he wasn't a traitor, Chester became extremely upset. "Jesus! Hobo, what have I done?"

Hobo tried to comfort him. "You had a setback. It happens to lots of people, but we'll make sure we get you back on track, and I'll be there for you. I promise."

Chester, growing more agitated, shook his head. "This goes way beyond falling off the wagon. My stupidity put everyone in this village in danger. I don't deserve to be here. I don't deserve the safety this place offers or to associate with the people here."

Jordan placed his hand over Chester's. "You screwed up royally, that's a fact, but that doesn't mean you don't deserve a safe home or friends. When people screw up or have a problem is when they need safety and friends the most. None of us are perfect. Sooner or later we all mess up in some way, but that doesn't have to define us. What defines us is whether or not we pick ourselves back up and what we do from there."

Chester squeezed the young man's hand, a tear making its way down his cheek. "I will pick myself up, and I will work hard to atone for what I did until I feel like I do deserve this place and these people."

Jordan smiled. "You already deserve it, but if that's how you need to look at it, that's fine. Whatever you need to do to stay sober and forgive yourself."

Hobo took Chester back to his house to begin working on a plan to ensure he got back on the right path, and JC left to run some tests on Mike. Gray and Jordan stayed behind to go over their notes from earlier in the day.

Gray groaned. "After getting a better look at that weapons and ammo cache, I feel like we have to hit that Danterford's today. If we're lucky, we should at least find a few rifles and more ammo there."

"Everyone should get proficient with bows and knives. They're much quieter."

"Agreed." Gray looked at Jordan across the table. "Listen, about earlier, I feel sympathy for Chester, but he did make a major mistake that could have affected many more people than just him. You let him off easy."

Jordan stopped writing but never put his pen down or looked up. "There are times when being tough on someone is the answer, and there are times when it isn't. I felt like this was one of the times it wasn't. Sometimes it's better to not kick someone while they're down."

Gray didn't say anything else, he just observed the young man across from him. In so many ways Jordan still seemed like a little boy, but in others, he seemed to have a wisdom far beyond his years. Gray didn't think that wisdom had only developed as a result of the apocalypse. As he watched Jordan start writing his notes again, he found himself again wondering what had happened to Jordan before the virus had been unleashed on the world. He was envious of Jordan's wisdom but felt certain he wouldn't envy whatever he had gone through to gain that wisdom.

Once they'd finished their notes and made copies for Hobo, they took his copies over to him at Chester's house.

Hobo thumbed through the notes. "You two have some excellent points in here. Looks like we have a lot of work to do. I have a list for you as well." He produced a folded paper from his back pocket and handed it over to Gray. "It's a list of the people I think would be the best candidates for the security team. I've already spoken with a few of them."

Gray noticed Chester sitting on the couch behind Hobo, still looking very remorseful and deflated. "Um, Hobo, you know, if we are going to grow and expand Sandbox, possibly establish outside posts and such, the power grid will need to be beefed up. I meant to make that suggestion before. To do that right we'll have to put the best person possible over it and trust them to train people to work under them. Whoever takes on that job will have many folks depending on them."

Hobo followed Gray's gaze to Chester, quickly realizing what Gray was doing. "I do believe you're right. We've always trusted Chester to keep the lights on for us. After all, he has the experience. I think he'd be the perfect man to lead the project."

Chester, who had been completely lost in his own thoughts and guilt until that point, looked at them with alarm etched all over his face. "Me? Oh, no! No, I am not the man for the job. I can't be trusted with it."

"So, you think you can't be trusted with a job that big yet," Jordan asked. "Okay, so be it, but you still need to help contribute around here. Maybe you'll rebuild some confidence in yourself as you do. We need to make a run, and we'll need several hands to grab and carry supplies. Why don't you start there?"

With Chester in tow, they recruited Paytan to go with them and were in the process of loading a pickup with the bags and crates for carrying loot when JC strolled by. He stopped to ask what they were doing. Once they told him, he insisted he would be accompanying them as he had some supplies he needed to pick up. Gray offered to get them for him, but JC declined, citing a need to do more than just survive. They needed to laugh and celebrate things. He knew if they didn't, they'd be no better off than the afflicted. They needed holidays spent in cozy homes, much like the ones in that tiny town, and they needed to venture outside their comfort zone from time to time.

Both trucks came to a stop a short distance from Danterford's. Jordan climbed into the bed of the pickup. With a pair of binoculars, he was able to see the exterior of Danterford's as well as the hospital directly across the road from Danterford's. It appeared the Danterford's had been secured almost as well as the one they'd briefly lived in with Kickz and the others back in Arizona. The fence wasn't quite as tall as the one in Arizona, but it was tall and sturdy enough to keep out afflicted. The parking lot was clear unlike the parking lot of the hospital where he counted at least a dozen or so afflicted stumbling around. He reported what he saw to the others. It was decided that they would leave the trucks parked there and stealthily make their way to Danterford's first so as not to draw too much attention. They would make sure Danterford's was clear, then clear the hospital, and then drive the trucks up to load whatever supplies they managed to find.

They were almost to Danterford's when a thought struck Jordan. "Guys, hold up. I think we should split up. I know it's risky, but if we hit Danterford's together and something goes wrong, say we make noise, we could attract the afflicted or anyone else that might be at the hospital. It could leave all of us wide-open to any number of things and maybe pinned down in Danterford's. Hitting both places at the same time may help us avoid that."

The others were hesitant to split up, but after weighing

the pros and cons they decided it would probably be for the best. Jordan, Gray, and Chester would go to the hospital while Hobo, JC, and Paytan went to Danterford's. The men wished each other luck and set off.

"Professor Jorgen, have you seen JC," Capp inquired upon entering the lab.

Jorgen looked up from his slides. "Not for a few hours. He mentioned needing some sort of special supplies. I believe he may have gone with Gray and some of the others on a supply run."

"Probably so, but I can't imagine the supplies we could get at any of the usual places, like Danterford's, would really be efficient for the type of work being done in this lab or with Mike."

Professor Jorgen took off his latex gloves. "You're very astute. For the time being, we have what we need, but that will change in just a matter of weeks. We've already begun thinking ahead to that time and considering our options. Our location may play in our favor. Being a military man yourself, I'm sure you know Virginia has several military facilities. Those facilities will probably have a great deal of what we need, but they will also probably be overrun with the afflicted, as you call them. We will need more muscle and firepower than we currently have to stand even a fraction of a chance of successfully getting in and out alive."

"Yeah, you have a point, but what does that have to do with JC going on a run today? Did they go to one of the facilities?"

"Oh, it has nothing to do with it, and I'm fairly certain they didn't go to any facilities. I just wanted to share the information with you and make sure you knew we had a plan since you brought up the subject of the supplies."

"Well, um, okay. I'll discuss it with JC and the rest of The Committee. We definitely have to make it a priority. The work going on here is too important. We can't let something like running out of supplies interfere with it."

"I'm glad you realize the importance of what we're doing here because I a favor to ask of you."

The tone of Jorgen's voice and his mannerism made Capp nervous. "When it comes to this research you need a favor? A favor from me?"

"Why is that so shocking?"

"Oh, I don't know. Maybe it's the fact you're the most intelligent person here. Hell, you're probably the most intelligent person I've ever met. And then there's the little matter of how you're supposed to be my teacher. All those things combined makes me wonder what I could possibly do to help you."

"Capp, I would appreciate it if you wouldn't underestimate yourself. You happen to possess a wide array of skills and wisdom that are beneficial to everyone here. As for helping me, you have a great deal more experience with the afflicted than I do. You know how to handle yourself around them, and I need one of them."

"Is that all? Why didn't you just say so? There's a few roaming around the woods outside the wall. I'll just put one down and bring it in. It'll only take a few minutes."

Jorgen shook his head. "I'm afraid I didn't express my

needs very well. I took many scans of Mike's brain, but I need two bases to compare it to. I need a living brain and the active brain of an afflicted."

Capp realized he'd been right to be nervous. "By active brain you mean you need a living afflicted."

Jorgen shrugged. "I'm not sure living is the proper term to use. That's why I said active. Basically, I need one that has not been damaged, so it can't be put down. Also, it goes without saying, we mustn't let anyone else see said afflicted."

Capp hung his head with a heavy sigh. "You don't want much, do you?"

After clearing the hospital parking lot Gray, Jordan, and Chester took a moment to analyze their options for the safest entry into the building. They first checked the front doors to the lobby and found they were locked.

"The doors are glass," Gray pointed out. "We could try to bust them, but I would bet they are incredibly thick, possibly bulletproof. The chances of us getting through are highly unlikely, and while we try, we'll make a lot of noise."

"Let's check the ER entrance," Jordan suggested.

To their disappointment, the emergency room entrance was also locked. Peering through the double sliding doors they could see a handful of afflicted wandering aimlessly. There were a couple of patients, a janitor, and a nurse. All of them looked rather nasty, but the nurse was particularly gruesome. Her right jaw was missing the flesh leaving her teeth, gums, and jawbone exposed. It somewhat resembled a disturbingly distorted half-grin, but her troubling appearance didn't end there. Her left eye dangled haplessly from its socket, bobbing and swaying with every shaky step she took. Even in that state, it was obvious she had once been a very attractive woman. The janitor, while still not a pleasant sight, was in much better shape than the nurse. They found him to be much more interesting than the nurse. Not because of his physical condition but because he had a set of keys dangling from his belt loop.

"Damn it," Gray exclaimed under his breath. "I bet those keys unlock every door here, including these. The universe is playing some sort of screwed up joke right now."

Jordan was staring at the keys. He thought he could hear them jingle as the janitor made his way across the room, but he knew it had to be his imagination as there was no way he could hear a sound no louder than that through those thick doors. He kept telling himself it was his imagination until he noticed the sound was getting louder, almost as if it was getting closer despite the janitor moving away from the doors. Suddenly he caught a glimpse of the reflection of an afflicted security guard on the glass. He swiftly spun around and drove his knife deep into the guard's eye. Gray and Chester, who had been unaware of the guard's presence, stood silently in stunned amazement.

Chester swallowed nervously. He swallowed so hard it was audible to the others. "I guess we should have checked around the outside better."

"We have to be more careful," Gray stated firmly. "As long as we've been living in this world now, we should be pros, and that was an amateur mistake!"

Jordan gave him a sly grin. “True that, but I think it may have been the universe showing us some mercy.” He bent down and removed a set of keys from the guard’s belt loop then proudly dangled them in front of Gray and Chester. “Thank you, universe.”

Equipped with the guard’s keys, the trio decided it would be best to find a side entrance, possibly one with fewer afflicted. They found such an entrance on the backside of the hospital. Although the building wasn’t very large in length or width it was four stories tall. For most towns it wouldn’t be considered a large facility at all, but Gray couldn’t help but notice it was overkill for such a tiny town and thought it to be odd. Once inside, he thought it was downright suspicious. As they made their way down the halls, checking rooms as they went, Gray was shocked by both the lack of afflicted and the high-end, advanced equipment. Some of the equipment was the kind of technology normally only found in the largest and finest hospitals or research facilities in the country. He wondered how it had found its way into a small hospital in the middle of nowhere.

“Something doesn’t feel right about this place,” he whispered to Jordan and Chester.

The three of them stopped in the middle of the hall.

Chester was relieved to hear Gray’s words. “I was thinking the same thing, but I don’t have a lot of experience doing this kind of thing, so I thought maybe I was just being paranoid. I thought there would be more dead in here. I mean, it is a hospital, shouldn’t there be more dead?”

"Exactly," Gray agreed, "and take a look at some of the equipment in here. It's far too advanced for a hospital like this. Then there's the size of this place."

"What about the size," Jordan asked.

"It's too big for a town this size," Gray answered. "Nothing about this place makes sense."

Jordan took a brief moment to ponder Gray's and Chester's points. "You're both right. I can't argue with you on any of it, but Sandbox needs medical supplies, and we're already here. Are you suggesting we should abort the mission?"

Gray's eyes darted around the hall. "Of course not. I just think we should be extra cautious."

They pushed on slowly, checking each room they came to. Most rooms were empty with the exception of one that was occupied by two afflicted. In the ER they put the patients, the janitor, and the pretty nurse out of their misery. Chester was taking the keys from the janitor when they heard the rustling of papers behind the nurse's station, instantly causing them to tense and hold their weapons a little higher. As the rustling continued, they carefully advanced toward it. Peering over the nurse's desk they saw a half-eaten afflicted dressed in military fatigues dragging himself across papers scattered on the floor. Gray made his way around the counter, his knife at the ready.

"Thank you for your service. It's time to rest now," he whispered before driving his knife into the man's ear. He turned to Jordan and Chester. "Why was he here? Why would the military have been here?"

"Maybe he was a local on leave," Chester speculated.

Gray looked down at the dead soldier. "I suppose that could have been the case, but why was he in fatigues if he was on leave?"

"We may never know," Jordan interjected. "What we do know is we have three more floors to go. Let's get it over with, this place is giving me the creeps."

The second floor was clear, and they found the third floor to be mostly clear save for an operating room that had been barricaded with furniture against the outside of the door. When they looked through the small window on one of the doors, they saw the room was full of afflicted, most of them being military personnel except for a couple of doctors and one patient. In total they counted around twenty afflicted contained in the room. They decided to deal with them after they cleared the fourth floor. They were making their way down a corridor on the fourth floor when Jordan abruptly threw his hand up, cuing Gray and Chester to stop.

"Did y'all hear that," Jordan asked.

Chester shook his head. "Hear what?"

Jordan strained to listen. "I'm not sure. It almost sounded like a baby crying."

"Maybe your mind is playing tricks on you," Gray proposed. "When we first came up here, we saw the maternity ward sign and the ultrasound machines sitting around. Maybe your imagination is taking that and running wild with it. Nobody could blame you. After all, this is sad and creepy as hell."

Nearly as soon as the words left his mouth, they all heard what sounded like a baby crying. It echoed throughout the otherwise deathly silent halls. It sent chills up their spines and filled them with dread. It was hard to determine where the sound was coming from. They moved down the hall, changing directions whenever the crying sounded as if it were getting farther away until they found themselves standing in an area where it sounded like they were right on top of it. For a moment they thought it was coming from one of the elevators next to them but quickly realized it was actually coming from a trash can sitting next to the elevators.

"Why the hell would a baby be in a garbage can," Chester asked breathlessly.

Jordan inched toward the trash can. He cautiously reached for the lid, but before he could grab it a cat flew out and landed at his feet. The men jumped back, but the cat calmly sat down, looked at them, and meowed in such a way it sounded very much like a baby crying.

Gray ran his hands through his hair in frustration. "Damned cat!"

His frustrated exclamation startled the feline almost as much as the feline had startled them. It bolted down the hall.

"Hey, hold on," Jordan called after it. "It's okay!" He proceeded to follow it, leaving Gray and Chester behind.

Chester watched him chase after the cat. "Is he really going after that demonic beast?"

Gray, still breathing heavily, nodded. "He's got a soft spot for animals."

"I normally do, but right now I want to kill that particular critter. My dad always said dogs were better than cats. Now I see he was right."

"I think I agree with your dad."

The temporary paralysis that had taken hold of

Chester's body subsided. He walked over to the trash can and gingerly ran his fingers over the top of it. "Gray, I would very much like to believe the sound we heard was that demonic ball of fur, I would truly like nothing more, but I can't. What we heard was a baby, not a cat."

"Chester, I know it sounded like a baby. To me a cat's cry has always sounded a little like a baby. Take a sound like that and put it in a metal garbage can in an abandoned hospital, and it will distort. That distortion in conjunction with our nerves may make it sound even more like a baby. It's really no wonder we thought that's what it was."

"I know that is the most reasonable explanation, but it doesn't feel right to me. I can't explain it, but something is just nagging at me."

Suddenly they heard Jordan calling to them. "Guys, come here. Quick!"

Both men rushed in the direction of the young man's voice. When they reached him, he was standing in front of a barricade comprised of such things as couches, beds, and filing cabinets.

"I wonder what's behind it," Chester mused.

Gray scanned the makeshift barricade before them. Something about it was off, but he couldn't quite put his finger on what it was.

Jordan pointed to a small gap at the bottom of the barricade between two filing cabinets. "The cat went through there."

Gray put his knife in its sheath before dropping down onto his stomach to look through the gap. "There's nothing back there but a wall."

Jordan was puzzled. "Then where did the cat go?"

Gray got to his feet and pointed to the filing cabinets. "Look at them compared to the rest of it. The rest has heavy furniture stacked a couple of layers thick, but not right there. In that spot there's nothing but the filing cabinets with a couple of boxes on top. They could easily be moved."

"Why would someone do that though," questioned Jordan. "If they were trying to hide a door I could see it, but a wall? Why would they barricade a wall in the first place? What good could it do?"

Gray started removing the boxes from the filing cabinets. "Help me."

Within a few seconds the three men had cleared away a large portion of the barricade around the area the cat disappeared. Just as Gray had said, there was a wall behind it and no sign of the mysterious cat.

Chester shook his head in confusion. "I'm with the kid. This makes no sense."

Gray's eyes remained trained on the wall. "It makes perfect sense."

"I think he's losing it," Jordan muttered to Chester.

"No, I'm not," Gray retorted, his eyes still focused on the wall. "That's raw drywall. This place has top of the line technology, nice furniture, and perfectly painted and decorated rooms. There's no way they would have left a wall unfinished. See that seam there? No tape, no mud, nothing," He pushed on the wall and felt it give way slightly. "There's something back there, but it's blocked. Cover me." With no further explanation he gave the wall a forceful kick and it swung open.

"How fresh does this specimen need to be," Capp asked as he and Jorgen trekked through the woods outside Sandbox.

Jorgen was fighting to free his shirt from a branch it had gotten snared on. "I will take whatever I can get, but truthfully, it would be better to have one that was reanimated around the same time as Mike was."

Capp grunted. "Reckon they carry around some sort of ID, but instead of a birthdate being listed it has a reanimated date?"

Jorgen, having freed himself from the branch, trailed a couple of feet behind Capp. "I detect sarcasm in your tone."

Capp laughed. "Sarcasm? Me? Why no! It's simple to look at these things and tell how long they've been turned. Same as telling the age of a tree by counting the rings. All we have to do is cut a leg off and count the rings. Better yet, we'll just ask them about that ID." He saw an afflicted a few yards ahead of them. "Let's ask her! Excuse me, Miss! Could you settle an argument for us?" He turned an ear toward her, pretending to listen to something she was saying. "What's that? Your name is Sylvia, and you'd be happy to help us. Well, that's awfully sweet of you, Sylvia. I'm Capp, and that's Professor Jorgen. We were wondering if you and your people happen to carry any kind of identification that might have your reanimated date on it."

"Capp, there is no need for this childish charade."

Capp ignored Jorgen. "No ID, Sylvia? Aww, that's

really too bad." He reached Sylvia and stabbed her in the eye. "That's really too bad. It would be helpful."

"Are you done now?"

Capp didn't acknowledge the question. "No ID, but she was too fresh anyway."

Jorgen caught up to Capp. "I can not only hear the frustration in your voice, I can feel it radiating off you."

Capp took a deep breath in an effort to calm himself. "Look, Professor, I'm sorry. I'm frustrated because you don't seem to realize what you're asking or how dangerous these things are. You've been behind that wall since this whole thing started. You haven't really seen what it's like to live among the afflicted. Have you ever seen one up close?"

"Other than Mike? No, I haven't, but that doesn't mean I don't understand. I've had friends leave the safety of our walls in search of supplies and never come back. I saw what happened insidc our walls when that poor woman's own child bit her. No, I didn't actually see it happen or see anyone turn, but I certainly saw the aftermath."

Capp softened. "I don't mean to diminish what you've experienced or disrespect the loss of your friends, but what you're talking about is a far cry from living out in the middle of this. It's very different from facing the afflicted daily."

"I know that, and that is part of why I asked for your help with this. I knew I didn't have the experience needed for this, and to be quite honest, I feel if I am going to truly help Mike or anyone else, I need this experience. I need to be able to understand it all on a firsthand level. As for determining someone's time of reanimation, under certain circumstances, I would be able to determine a general age if you will.

Unfortunately, we are far from those circumstances. The heat, humidity, and insect activity they are exposed to every day makes it impossible for me to even get close to an accurate date of their turning. I am a very intelligent man in many areas, I know that. It's not arrogance, it's simply a fact, but I am completely ignorant in other areas, particularly world and life experience. You, on the other hand, are not. I'd hoped your knowledge in those areas might have helped you develop a way, an intuition, or something to allow you to estimate how long they'd been turned. Perhaps my reasoning was flawed."

Capp felt bad for being so harsh with him. "Yeah, well, if we get one, you can use it to help Mike and formulate a way to estimate when they turned. Maybe with one in captivity you can study its decomposition rate or something."

"I could. I am certain with the help of some of my best students, yourself included, I could absolutely develop something. The knowledge that could be gained by capturing one of them could be invaluable in a variety of ways."

"I can agree with you on that. I can also agree to you needing the experience, I have an idea to get you that experience, but first, let's take care of securing your specimen."

Gray, Jordan, and Chester exchanged bewildered glances before looking back to the wall which was open just enough for them to see there was an open space behind it. They crept forward warily with their weapons at the ready. Stepping into the space behind the wall, they discovered a pair of doors that seemingly led to another wing. Chester pushed one of the doors open, and immediately they heard the baby crying again.

"I'm going to strangle that damn cat if we find it," Gray whispered.

"We don't know who is back here. Somebody set all of this up for a reason. For all we know, there could be somebody in here with an actual baby," Chester cautioned.

With that in mind, they crept silently down the hall. They could hear the crying growing louder until they reached a closed door the sound seemed to be emanating from, along with a voice.

"Shh, you have to be quiet now. Be quiet or they'll find us, the voice softly warned.

Gray swapped his knife for his pistol and motioned to Jordan and Chester to do the same. Jordan readied himself to open the door from the side while Gray and Chester positioned themselves in front of it, ready to open fire if necessary. Gray held up three fingers to count down. When his last finger went down Jordan flung the door open. Inside they saw a frightened man in scrubs backed into a corner on the far side of the room. In his arms was the cat.

"Please, don't hurt us," he pleaded.

Gray took a step into the room. "We don't intend to unless you get stupid. You're not a stupid man, are you?"

"No, I'm not. At least I don't think I am. I'm Doctor Patrick Popal, and this is..." He looked at the cat and hesitated. "Well, I don't really know who this is. I never gave him a name.

Pretty bad of me, huh? The only companion I've had for months, and I never gave him a name."

"What are you doing here," Jordan demanded. "Did you put up that barricade and the false wall?"

"Yes, that was my doing. I saw someone put up a false wall like that in a movie once, and..."

Jordan cut him off. "Dawn of the Dead. It was one of my mom's favorites."

Dr. Popal smiled. "Yes! Romero, nineteen seventy-eight, if I recall correctly." He noticed Gray didn't appear to be enjoying the movie trivia. "As I was saying, I've been surviving here for some time, and I found a room up here with a bunch of drywall sheets, paint, and things like that. Apparently, they were getting ready to do some remodeling to the hospital when the world fell. I remembered the movie and decided it might not be such a bad idea. Figured it would be extra protection from any unscrupulous living as well as the walkers."

Jordan chuckled. "Walkers, huh? Is that what you call them? Let me guess you, were a Walking Dead fan too."

Popal blushed. "I won't deny it. I guess you could say I was a connoisseur of all things zombie. Taking that into consideration, you'd think I would have been more prepared for the apocalypse. You know, when I watched The Walking Dead, I used to imagine, if an apocalypse ever happened, I'd be a badass, Rick Grimes, type. That's what I wanted to believe but turns out I'm more of a Eugene Porter type."

"The world needs both types." Jordan assured him.

Gray wasn't ready to let his guard down with the chatty, awkward doctor. "You said you found the room with the drywall in it, if you're a doctor, you should have known the hospital you worked in was having work done."

"I am a doctor, but this was never the hospital I worked at. I worked under this hospital."

The doctor's answer surprised and befuddled Gray. "What the hell?"

Capp struggled to keep his grip on the afflicted he and Jorgen had selected. It was a male roughly the same size and age as Mike. Its strength amazed Capp.

"Hey, Professor, I'd say now would be a good time to get your ass over here with that sack and those zip ties! I feel like I'm fighting a bull here."

Jorgen looked down at the burlap sack and zip ties in his hands. Their plan had been that Capp would get an afflicted under control, and the professor would throw the sack over its head to prevent biting then bind its hands together with the zip ties to prevent it from grabbing at them and flailing around so much. When they'd first discussed it, Jorgen thought it was a solid plan and was confident he could uphold his end of it. Now, face to face with the afflicted man, his confidence was nowhere to be found. His fear and repulsion froze him to the spot where he stood.

"Professor Jorgen, snap out of it," Capp commanded. "I really don't want to get bit. I need you! Mike needs this afflicted! The future of humanity could very well depend on your research, research that is dependent on this afflicted man!"

Capp's words got through to something within Jorgen. With no thought at all, his body was in motion. He flung the sack over the afflicted's head, and after a brief scuffle, he managed to get the hands secured. The afflicted man was still strong and still struggled, but he was slightly easier to control.

"Now all we have to do is figure out how we're going to get him into Sandbox without anyone seeing him. We didn't think that part through, Professor."

Jorgen snickered. "I think I know how. I probably should have thought of it much sooner. It would have been so much easier and faster. Do you still have your knife handy?"

Capp patted the knife on his hip. "Always."

"Good. Hold him down and give me your knife."

Capp wrestled the afflicted onto the ground and straddled its chest. "Now what?"

Jorgen removed the sack from the dead man's head and shoved it into the man's mouth, being careful to avoid being bitten. "Capp, close your eyes and your mouth. You don't want to get any of it in either one."

"Any of what?"

Jorgen hastily began to cut along the afflicted's throat in a sawing motion. Dark blood spilled onto the ground. "Ah, yes, I should have taken into consideration the heart isn't beating. No beating heart, no blood pressure. No blood pressure, no spurting. No spurting, no worries of getting blood in your mouth or eyes."

Capp grimaced. "What are you doing?"

"Sooner or later, I will need a whole specimen, but

for now, the head will suffice, and a head in a bag will be much easier to get inside the wall unseen."

The afflicted man jerked and struggled in a manner uncharacteristic of the dead. The movement startled Jorgen and Capp. The dead man's mouth moved in such a way it appeared to be trying to scream, and his eyes no longer looked like those of a soulless, bloodthirsty monster. Instead, its eyes looked filled with fear.

Jorgen's hand began to shake. "Oh, dear God! Do you think it feels this? Does it feel pain?"

The implications were not lost on Capp, and he felt sick. "I... I don't know! Just finish it fast!"

Jorgen worked as quickly as possible. He wanted the task over with as much for the dead man's sake as his and Capp's. After the head was completely detached, it remained animated while the body was lifeless. The eyes of the dead man returned to the usual look they'd come to expect of the afflicted.

"Maybe we just imagined it. It was a stressful situation." Jorgen reasoned. "It's been proven stress can do a number of things to the mind."

"That's what it was," Capp said somberly. "That's what it had to be."

They carefully removed the sack from the mouth of the afflicted head then crammed the head into the sack and began making their way back to the Sandbox drawbridge. They walked in silence, but they were both thinking the same thing, it hadn't been their imagination.

They were back inside the walls of Sandbox a short time later. Several people passed them, some even saying hello, but none noticed the sack Jorgen carried was moving. They were within a few feet of the lab when Bobby strolled by them. He nodded and smiled in greeting. Jorgen and Capp thought they were in the clear, but then Bobby glanced at the sack.

"Whatever you've got in there doesn't seem so happy about the accommodations." Bobby pointed to the sack. "It's doing a lot of squirming."

Capp's mind raced to come up with a plausible explanation. "Uh, yeah, it's a possum."

Jorgen cut his eyes toward Capp but decided to roll with it. "Yes, a possum. We caught a possum."

Bobby was delighted. "We've been running low on meat, and although possum is an acquired taste, when done right, it can be quite tasty. I have a marvelous recipe for possum stew. If you'll give it to me, I will dispatch the critter, humanely of course, and get to cooking."

Jorgen shrank back from Bobby's outstretched hand. "I would, but this possum is special. We, uh..."

"We believe it's pregnant," Capp blurted. "We believe it's pregnant, and we thought we could let it have its babies here, raise them, and breed them once we catch a few more. You know, start a self-sustaining meat supply. The Professor was just going to examine it, make sure it's healthy."

"That is wonderful," Bobby exclaimed. "Very smart thinking, gentlemen. Do let me know if I can help."

Capp nervously chuckled. "Sure thing."

Bobby gave them another smile and went about his way.

"Nice save," Jorgen told Capp in a hushed voice. "However, I will never eat possum stew."

Hobo, JC, and Paytan stepped out of Danterford's and into the parking lot. The sun was blindingly bright after being in the dark store.

Hobo squinted as he looked to the hospital across the road. "Shouldn't they be done over there by now?"

"They did have more floors to clear," Paytan pointed out.

"That's true but considering the dimensions of the hospital versus Danterford's they really didn't have much more square footage to cover than we did though. Could mean they had more afflicted to clear. If we really look at it, the hospital being unsecured along with the very fact it is a hospital it would stand to reason the odds of there being an increased number of afflicted would be elevated. That having been said, they are more than capable of handling themselves. I'm positive they are fine, but things would go much faster if they had help."

Hobo flashed JC a playful smirk because he knew JC was making excuses to go check on them.

"This is the only unlocked door," Hobo informed JC and Paytan. He slowly pulled the door open. "I didn't see any broken windows or anything like that. They had to have gone through here."

They stepped through the door and navigated the halls of the hospital's first floor, eventually coming across the emergency room.

Paytan shined his flashlight across the bodies of the afflicted scattered around the nurse's desk. "Looks like they definitely came through here." He continued to scan the rest of the area. The beam of his flashlight reflected off something by the elevators. It was a small sign on a door. "Hey, guys, I think I just found the door to the basement."

JC's gaze followed the beam of light. "Likely a boiler room or maintenance area down there. There might be some generators and other useful things down there. We can kill two birds with one stone, check for the others and scope out possible loot. If we don't find them down there, then we'll head upstairs."

Gray paced the floor in front of the table Jordan, Chester, and Dr. Popal sat at. His frustration was evident in both the expression on his face and the tone of his voice. "Let me get this straight, you're telling us there is some sort of entire facility under this hospital."

"Not just under the hospital," Popal corrected. "It runs under the entire town."

Gray stopped pacing. "That's right, a facility as big as a small town completely underground. Nobody knew about it? Not one soul knew about something that big?"

"I never said that. I didn't even imply that. What I said was very few knew about it."

Gray bit his bottom lip, looked up at the ceiling, and huffed before pulling a chair over to the table and sitting down. "Okay, I want to hear your story again, from the beginning."

Popal took a sip from his water bottle and launched into his story. He had worked for a rather large company that had been founded in the fifties by a well-to-do family that included the likes of senators, mayors, doctors, and lawyers. Rumor had it several members of the family had been regulars on the guest lists of parties thrown by the Kennedys. The company originally specialized in bath and skin care products, but in the late sixties it expanded into household cleaners. By the eighties the company had its hands in a little bit of everything, including medicinal development. At that time, the town they were currently in was even smaller. It mainly consisted of a handful of homes, one gas station, and a small general store. The pawnshop, Danterford's, and the hospital didn't exist, but a bunker underneath where the hospital now stood had existed.

Back then the bunker had been small, just big enough for a dozen or so people. It had been built in the late fifties, during the Cold War, specifically for the family that founded the company. They, like many during that period, had felt certain the former Soviet Union would drop a nuclear warhead on the United States, and they intended to ride out the aftermath in the bunker. Although the Cold War didn't end until the early nineties, the family decided in nineteen eighty-four the threat of a nuclear attack was low enough they no longer needed the bunker, but rather than do away with it or abandon it, they decided to repurpose it. The company had just accepted government contracts to develop things such as vaccines, prosthetics, and various medical procedures. The family, being distrustful of everyone, felt the need to keep such work a secret and as secure as possible, and the old bunker gave them an idea of how to do just that. If they could have a self-sustaining bunker for twelve people, why couldn't they have a self-sustaining lab and work community underground?

With that in mind, they had plans drawn up with the original bunker as the main entrance to an underground complex. They then set about buying up all the property in town. The town's residents and business owners were perplexed as to why such a large and well-known company would be interested in their little town, but when the company's representatives waved checks for nearly quadruple what their properties were worth in front of them, they stopped asking questions and started packing.

From there it was a simple matter of finding contractors and employees the company could trust, starting construction, and deciding what to do with the town itself. The right amount of money and nondisclosure agreements was enough to secure the silence and loyalty of contractors and employees at which point construction began, leaving only the issue of what to do with the town. One member of the founding family was a psychiatrist, and he worried about the mental health of employees living and working underground year-round. He suggested leaving the town standing and adding new structures and businesses. He reasoned it would serve as added security and camouflage for the underground complex while keeping the employees' mental health in a good state because they would have access to aboveground activities, and most importantly, they would have a sense of normalcy and community.

Everyone involved thought it was a brilliant idea. To avoid suspicion from outsiders they decided to keep the town small and make it resemble other towns in the area as much as possible. To further give the town the appearance of an ordinary town, the spouses and other family members of employees were hired to do jobs within the town such as running the new grocery store or working at the new hospital, which was built directly on top of the original bunker. No one would suspect the town was anything other than a quaint, rural town on a back road in Virginia.

Jordan was awed. “A whole town built by one company and run by its people with a giant secret right below their feet. Sounds too incredible to be true.”

“Young man, the right amount of money can make almost anything possible,” Popal responded. “Since that time, most of the children of those original employees and families have grown up, had families of their own, gone to work for the company, and stayed here in this town. I was one of those children. The company even paid for my college education.”

Gray stood and started to pace again. “I grew up not far from here, and there’s always talk and rumors about everything in small towns. Folks can be kind of nosy in little towns, and they all love a good conspiracy. The thing about rumors and conspiracies is they tend to spread like wildfire. I never heard anything about this town. Forgive me if I find it hard to swallow. Can we see this mysterious, underground facility? If you didn’t work in this hospital, why are you in here? Why was the military here?”

Popal’s face reflected the pain and sorrow he felt. “While I chose to live in one of the houses in town and occasionally consulted on patient cases here in the hospital, I worked in the complex below. Several months before the outbreak began, the government sent the military here because we were working on identifying a strange biological substance found on a foreign operative. When the outbreak started, I was in the hospital visiting a doctor friend on one of my breaks. We were sitting in this room, just sipping coffee and making plans for a fishing trip, when we heard a scream from down the hall. We rushed down the hall. People were running in all directions, some were utterly hysterical, and then we saw it. There was a child, no more than eight years old, ripping flesh from a pregnant woman's arm with his teeth. Within minutes soldiers started rushing people down to the complex. Some soldiers stayed down there with us to be a line of defense if we were breached, but the majority of them remained topside and attempted to defend the town. There are cameras hidden all over the town with access to the live feed in the complex, so we were able to monitor everything happening topside. The soldiers managed to hold their own at first, but about three days in a large horde came through. There were so many of them, too many of them. When the dust settled, I watched as one young soldier stumbled out of the pharmacy in town. I could see he was limping and disoriented. It was clear he couldn't make it down to us on his own so, I convinced three soldiers to go topside with me to retrieve him. It was a hazardous mission to say the least, but we were successful. Once we had him below, we discovered he had a ferociously high fever and a bite on his leg. We cleaned, sterilized, and stitched the bite then turned our attention to lowering his fever."

"What the hell were you thinking," Chester spat. "Why didn't you put him down?"

Popal turned to him with tear-filled eyes. "You have to understand, it was the beginning of the outbreak. We didn't know for certain what the walkers were or what their bites would do. We were doing the best we could with the knowledge we had at the time, which was basically none. Yes, I was a zombie fan, but I never thought I'd be in the middle of a zombie apocalypse! Did you? When you first saw them did your mind automatically jump to zombie?"

Chester shook his head somberly.

Popal continued with his story. "We got him as stable as we could, but he died in the middle of the night. His commanding officer had been sitting with him and fell asleep. The young man turned and attacked the sleeping officer. After that it was a domino effect. I managed to get out with Doctor Monroe, and we shut the bunker and stacked boxes in front of the bunker door in the hospital's basement. Our first thought was to get a vehicle and flee, but the moment we stepped onto the first floor by the emergency room, it was clear things weren't going to go as planned. There weren't a lot of dead there, but the ones that were stood between us and the exit. Doctor Monroe recognized one of them, a nurse. She tried to talk to her, to reason with her. Of course, it didn't work, and Doctor Monroe was bitten. I don't know how I did it, but I managed to get the nurse off her and pulled Doctor Monroe into the elevator. That's when we came up here."

"Then what," Gray questioned. "You cleared all but the first floor of the hospital by yourself? With a bit woman in tow?

Oh, and let's not forget the operating room full of afflicted. Suppose you did that by yourself too? Do you see the issues I'm having with this? You've just told us this story about this fantastical and creepy town with an equally creepy underground complex, which by the way, I'm getting some serious Raccoon City vibes off that shit, and now this!"

Jordan snickered, "Maybe the company he keeps talking about is Umbrella," he joked with a mischievous grin.

Gray glared at him. "Not the time, Jordan." He directed his attention back to Popal. "But since he brought it up, what about that? Was this company of yours some sort of Umbrella wannabe?"

"No, absolutely not!" Popal sighed. "I get it, you're suspicious. You think I'm up to something or hiding something. I didn't have to do any clearing to the upper floors because the soldiers had already done it. They'd started clearing this place before they were overrun. They probably locked all those dead in that operating room because they didn't understand what they were then. They probably thought they were just sick or crazy. Doctor Monroe and I came straight to the fourth floor. I tried to stabilize her, but it was useless. She had a deep bite on her neck and bled out rather quickly. I covered her with a sheet and started looking for things I could use to defend myself. I was passing back by the room where I'd left her and heard noises. For a minute I thought perhaps in my panic and destress, I'd pronounced her dead too hastily. However, when I opened the door, I realized she'd turned. She lunged at me, and I impaled her with an IV pole. To my horror, she kept coming."

"Did you figure out how to put her down?" Chester asked.

Popal stared at his hands in his lap. "That moment was the first time I allowed the thought they might be zombies to cross my mind. Being a fan of things such as The Walking Dead and people such as George Romero, it was natural for the next thought to be to aim for the head. That was what I intended to do, but... I... I just couldn't. She was a colleague and a friend. I couldn't do it."

Gray's frustration boiled over. "You're telling us she is still wandering around this hospital? What the hell is wrong with you? Are you crazy? Have you completely lost your marbles? For someone so smart, you're sure dumb! Why didn't you mention this sooner? You put us all in danger by not sharing that little tidbit!"

Doctor Popal wrung his hands. "I know it was stupid! I know what I should have done, but I simply couldn't!"

Leaning down to get on eye level with the doctor, Gray placed a fist, knuckles down, on the table. "What did you do? Where is she?"

Before Popal could answer, a sound echoing from somewhere in the hospital rattled them all. It was crying, a baby crying. Gray, Jordan, and Chester glanced around the room in search of the cat. It was sunbathing silently in the window. Everyone was shocked, apart from the doctor.

"We heard that earlier and thought it was the cat. It wasn't though, was it," Jordan asked Popal. "You know what it is, don't you?"

Popal replied with a solemn gaze and a nod.

JC shoved bandages into his bag. "I'm not complaining." He grabbed more bandages from the shelf. "We can use everything we've found down here, but I am troubled by one thing."

"What's that," Hobo asked as he filled his bag with bottles of rubbing alcohol.

JC shone his flashlight around the room. "This basement doesn't make sense to me. I wouldn't think hospitals would keep supplies in the basement because basements normally aren't sterile environments. Supplies like these should be kept in a sterile environment."

Paytan looked around and shrugged. "This place is cleaner than most people's houses."

"That's my point! It's too clean for a basement. Something feels off about it."

Hobo stopped packing his bag to take a better look at the room himself. "I hate to say it, JC, but I have to disagree with you on this one. The hospital in my hometown in Canada had a morgue, a lab, and a few exam rooms in the basement. It was every bit as clean as this."

"I respect your opinion, Hobo, but I cannot ignore my instinct. A hospital with things like that in the basement would be very clean because it wasn't a normal basement. There is nothing like that in this particular basement. There's only a maintenance office, maintenance supply room, a machinery room, and this random room full of what should be sterile supplies, and the floors are so clean you could eat off of them."

From the other side of the room, Paytan called to them. "Guys, look at this stack of boxes. Some of them are labeled. Looks like more bandages, gauze, peroxide, and a few other things. Mostly all stuff we can use, but a couple aren't labeled. Let's see what's in this one." He pulled a box toward him and started tugging on the top but stopped when he caught a glimpse of something behind the boxes. "Uh, I think you should come look at this."

JC and Hobo joined Paytan and saw what appeared to be a thick, metal door behind the boxes.

"What do you think is behind it," Paytan asked.

"Only one way to find out," JC answered. "Make sure you have your weapons ready gentlemen."

Gray and Chester couldn't take their eyes off the scene in the nursery before them. Jordan and Doctor Popal couldn't bear to continue looking and turned away. On the other side of the nursery window, Doctor Monroe stood over a bassinet, gazing down at a crying, afflicted infant.

"She looks almost worried for the baby," Chester whispered, his eyes still fixed on Doctor Monroe. Upon seeing her tenderly stroke the tiny afflicted's head with her stiff, jerking hand, he was so shaken he involuntarily took a few steps back. "What the hell is she doing? Did y'all see that?"

Jordan forced himself to turn around. He felt a lump in his throat as he watched her try to comfort the poor baby. "She's like Mike. Maybe the baby is too. It is responding to her touch, it's calming down."

Gray's head instantly whipped around to cast a stern glare at Jordan. "Enough!"

Chester looked back and forth between them. "What are you two talking about? Did you say something about Mike? What about Mike?"

"Chester, not now," Gray firmly told him before turning his stern glare to Popal who was pacing behind them. "How the hell did this situation come about?" He got no response from Popal who simply continued to pace which served to enrage Gray. "You son of a bitch, what did you do," Gray shouted, rushing towards Popal and forcefully shoving him into the wall. "Did you let her bite that baby? Answer me, or I'll put you in that room with her!"

Doctor Popal recoiled. "No! Please, no! I didn't! I wouldn't!"

Jordan stepped between the two men. "It's okay," He calmly assured the doctor. "Just take a deep breath and tell us what happened."

Popal moved to the nursery window. For the first time since he'd led the men there, he looked into the nursery. "As I told you before, I knew what I should have done with her. I feel guilty for not doing so. She was a good person and deserved so much better than this. I simply couldn't bring myself to do the right thing. We were in a room not far down the hall from this nursery. She was reaching for me, pulling at my clothes, and that's when I first heard the crying. She heard it too."

"How did she end up out of that room and in this nursery," Chester demanded. "And why does she act that way?"

Popal continued to watch Doctor Monroe. “She lost all interest in me when she heard the crying. She started moving toward the sound. I was terrified there was a living baby in there. I mean it didn’t sound exactly natural, and I suspected it wasn’t a normal baby, but I wasn’t willing to take the chance. I ran down the hall past her. Looking through this window I could see it wasn’t a living child, but I needed to be absolutely certain. I went in there. I checked all the other bassinets first, to be sure there were no other babies, before I went to that one. There was no doubt that baby had turned. I checked for bites, but there weren’t any. I could find no reason at all for that baby to be the way it was or why it had been left behind. My heart broke for it, and apparently Doctor Monroe’s did as well. By then, she was clawing at the door, desperate to get to the crying baby. Part of me thought maybe it was wrong to let her in because I didn’t know if she would hurt it. Even in that state, it was still a baby, and it seemed so wrong to risk her hurting it. On the other hand, we hadn’t seen any indications they would harm each other, and to be perfectly honest, the scientist in me had noticed the change in her demeanor when she heard the crying. That part of me very much wanted to see how she would react to the child.”

Jordan was disturbed by the thought of Popal letting Doctor Monroe into the nursery, but he couldn’t deny, had he been the one in that situation, he would have been equally as curious as Popal had been. “So, you let her in?”

“I did. She didn’t even seem to realize I was there. The pole was still protruding from her, and I knew it would hinder her movement around the room and possibly her interaction with the baby, so I grabbed the end of it and pulled as hard as I could. It took a few tries, but I finally got it out. She still never acknowledged my presence. As far as she was concerned, nothing existed but that baby, and once she was free, she went straight to it. There was an empty bottle lying in the bassinet with the baby. She picked it up and tried to give it to the baby. I was frozen. I couldn't stop watching even though I knew I needed to get out of there. I guess my survival instinct overrode my fascination because, without making the conscious decision to do so, I quietly slipped out and shut the door behind me. They've been in there ever since."

For several minutes they all stood in complete silence, watched Doctor Monroe and the baby, and tried to digest what they'd just been told. It was Jordan who finally broke the silence.

"Doc, I understand the position you were in and why you did what you did, but I have some questions. First off, wouldn't that pole have ripped her and her clothes up pretty good, both going in and coming out? She looks like she's in pretty good condition and has on clean scrubs. Then there's the general overall condition of her and the baby. They're both in good condition to be what they are. If they've been in there all this time, then they haven't been able to feed. Wouldn't starvation have affected their condition?"

Popal fidgeted nervously with the drawstring on his scrubs. "I can provide the answers you seek. As for the damage the pole caused, well, I stitched her up. You see, as long as Timothy is crying, all of her focus is on him."

Gray interrupted him. "Wait! Timothy?"

Popal pointed to the baby. "The information card on his bassinet had Timothy listed as his name. As I was saying, when he cries, she focuses on nothing but him. After a couple of days, I couldn't stand seeing her like that anymore. While she was distracted with Timothy, I rolled a stretcher in and threw a sheet over her from behind. It took a little wrestling, but I managed to get her secured to the stretcher. I sewed her up and bathed her before putting a fresh set of scrubs on her. Before I released her, I gave Timothy a bath and found a little sleeper to put on him. I know how ridiculous it sounds, but they'd both been let down by everyone. They deserved at least that. Now we do the bath thing around once every two weeks. As for why they aren't starving, they should be. They probably would be if I hadn't started feeding them."

Gray huffed and rolled his eyes. "I should be shocked, but after everything else, somehow, I'm just not. I would like to know exactly what you've been feeding them though."

"In the beginning it was meat from Danterford's. Their coolers and freezers are hooked into the bunker grid, so they still had power. I was worried they would only accept living flesh, but I found as long as I got the meat to room temperature, they ate it. The problem came a couple of weeks later when I noticed they were slowing down. It was as if the meat was keeping them going but only barely. I still refused to give them anything living or human, but I thought maybe fresher meat would work better. I helped myself to a rifle and ammunition from Danterford's and started hunting. I'd never hunted in my life until then, and I was a terrible shot, but I got better. I mostly came back with small game, but I managed to get a deer a couple of times. I began giving them small portions of the fresh meat or mixing it with the meat from Danterford's to make it go further, and they improved. Doctor Monroe became more docile, and Timothy cried less and less. Considering that, I decided since we had nothing but time, we might as well see if we could make progress on their behavior, particularly Doctor Monroe's. Incredibly, she made great progress. You should have seen it."

"We have seen it," Jordan muttered under his breath.

Gray's instinct was to reprimand him but fearing it would only draw more questions from Chester, he chose to quickly change the subject instead. "Doctor, I was under the impression you hadn't left this building. How were you getting out? Did you go through the afflicted downstairs every time you left?"

"Oh, certainly not. I'm not brave enough for that. I come and go through the window in the room where you found me. I use an emergency fire ladder, one of those that folds up and hooks onto the window. I always put the cat in the bathroom before I do. Can't have him hurting himself jumping out."

Gunshots suddenly rang out from one of the lower floors. They heard voices between the shots.

Jordan listened closely to the voices. "I'm pretty sure one of those voices is Hobo."

"I think I heard JC too," Gray added. "They probably came looking for us, but what are they shooting at?"

"Popal rushed to push a stretcher in front of the nursery door, explaining the door was locked, but he wanted an extra layer of protection between Doctor

Monroe and Timothy and whatever might be in the building. Gray instructed the doctor to lock himself in the bathroom with the cat and to not come out until one of them came to get him. Gray, Jordan, and Chester then went to the stairwell door. Gray was about to open the door when it was flung open, and JC, Hobo, and Paytan rushed through it.

"Quick," JC yelled, "find a way to barricade that door!"

Hearing the sound of multiple afflicted on the stairs, Gray wasted no time in rolling a hospital bed in front of the door. "Find stuff to stack on this," he ordered over his shoulder.

The others scattered, gathering anything they could stack on the bed. In a matter of moments, they'd piled filing cabinets, chairs, and garbage cans on it. When they thought they'd done enough, they stopped to collect themselves, and Chester retrieved Popal from the bathroom.

"Y'all, that door opens out into the stairwell," Jordan observed. "It's not like they could push it open."

JC laughed. "Your observation is correct, and yes, our efforts were essentially useless, but I must admit, I feel better with that stuff between us and them."

"Absolutely feel better, safer," Chester agreed. "It does create another issue though. Now we're trapped on this floor."

"Are those the afflicted from the operating room on the third floor," Gray inquired.

"Third floor," Hobo asked in confusion. "We never saw the third floor. We opened a weird door in the basement, almost like a vault door, and a whole damned horde came out. We hauled biscuits up those stairs and straight up here. This was no normal hospital."

Gray cast a side glance at Doctor Popal. “You have no idea.”

Until then, Hobo hadn’t noticed the doctor. “Who is he?”

“I’ll explain on the way to get help from Sandbox,” Gray answered. “We need to clear this hospital and the town. Then we need to secure it all.”

“This is all very interesting, and if you say that is what needs to be done, I trust you, but as Chester mentioned, we’re just a little trapped up here,” JC pointed out.

Gray smirked. “Chester is forgetting something the good doctor told us earlier.”

A knowing expression fell over Chester’s face. “The ladder!”

The noise from the agitated afflicted on the other side of the door was growing louder.

Shifting from foot to foot, Jordan stared at the door. “Yeah, kinda thinking it’s time we introduce ourselves to that ladder.”

Without hesitation, they hastily followed Doctor Popal to the window he used as an entrance and exit. He swiftly retrieved his ladder and attached it to the window. It was obvious he’d done it many times before. He then made certain his cat was in the room with them before closing the door and placing the table and some chairs against it.

Doctor Popal turned to the other men who were watching him. “Why are you still here? Go! Get down the ladder and bring help back!”

“You’re coming with us,” Jordan informed him, a

noticeable sternness in his voice.

"I can't. I won't leave Doctor Monroe and Timothy." He looked over to the happily oblivious cat grooming himself. "Not to mention him. Gray is right, this facility and town need to be taken back from the dead and protected from any amoral living so, please, go! Go bring back people to help do that!"

Jordan picked up the cat, cradled it in his arms, and stroked its back. "Gray, we'll be right here when you get back, but make it sorta quick if you don't mind."

"Who are Doctor Monroe and Timothy," JC queried.

Gray nodded to Jordan then turned to JC. "Two people you're definitely going to want to meet. I'll explain along the way.

Gray made sure Chester and Paytan were in one truck while JC and Hobo were in the other with him. He wanted the time alone with them to explain everything they'd found at the hospital.

JC was astonished. "You're telling me not only is there an entire research facility under that town, but they also have a woman and an infant like Mike?"

Gray shrugged. "Pretty much."

Hobo exhaled sharply. "The world keeps getting stranger and stranger. To think, I used to complain about how boring my life was."

"One other thing," Gray began. "Jordan was rattled when he saw Doctor Monroe and Timothy, and he might have mentioned Mike in front of Doctor Popal and Chester."

Hobo hung his head. "That could throw a big ole monkey

wrench in the works. I would kill for a Hobo cookie right now."

"No worries, gentlemen," JC reassured them. "Chester is a good man. We will have to explain it to him and trust him to do the right thing. As for Doctor Popal, all things considered, I believe he will understand the need for discretion and be a valuable ally. My only concern is others we are about to take back with us to clear the hospital might see Doctor Monroe or Timothy. Other than that, I am most excited by the opportunity to get to know Doctor Popal and meet Doctor Monroe and Timothy."

Upon arrival at Sandbox, they gave Capp a rundown of everything that had transpired. Capp was conflicted. Part of him was almost fearful of what was going on at the hospital. Since the virus had been released, he'd seen terrifying and fantastical things, but they were almost tame in comparison to what he'd just been told. Yet his inquisitive mind was slightly more excited than fearful.

Jordan and Doctor Popal were chatting about normal things, the kinds of things people talked about before the world fell, when they heard shots in the hospital.

Popal got excited. "Your friends are back!"

Jordan drew his pistol. "Probably, but there is a possibility it could be someone else."

"You mean the people in the trucks? The crazy ones? I've seen them around before. I think they've been looking for someone."

Jordan started moving the table and chairs away

from the door. "Sounds like we might be talking about the same folks."

"If you are worried about those people, why are you removing the furniture from the door? Shouldn't we leave it there?"

"Look, no matter who is out there, we have two people down the hall that don't need to be seen by anyone yet. If some of our people see Doctor Monroe and the baby they might put them down out of instinct. If the crazy people see them, almost guaranteed they will put them down." A thought suddenly occurred to him. "Timothy doesn't have teeth. How do you feed him?"

"I puree his meat, add a little formula to it, and put it in a bottle. I've been adding the formula to see how his body reacts to it and attempt to get it accustomed to having the type of food and nutrients a normal baby's body should have."

"Okay, okay. Does Doctor Monroe give it to him? If she does, does she remain focused on him while she does?"

"Sometimes I give him a bottle, but most of the time she does, and yes, she is totally focused on him when she does. I actually sat a bottle out to warm up for him right before you guys found me."

"Very good. Here's what we're going to do. We're going to go give Doctor Monroe the bottle for a couple of reasons. For one, it should keep Timothy from crying. He needs to be quiet until we know who is in the hospital. For another, it will keep her occupied while we close the nursery curtains. After we get them closed, we pile a few things in front of the door, and then we hide in one of the rooms close to the nursery where we can keep eyes on them and protect them if necessary. Think you can handle it?"

Popal nodded nervously.

Jordan wasn't reassured by it. "Doc, if you can't, it's fine. I'll go by myself. There can't be any hesitation out there, and we have to be swift. If you can't do that then it's safer for me, Doctor Monroe, and Timothy if I go alone."

Popal stood a little straighter. "I can do this."

Jordan led the way to the nursery. They were relieved when they didn't encounter any living or dead along the way. After rolling away the stretcher in front of the nursery door, Popal fumbled to get the key into the lock, dropping it twice.

"Take a deep breath and steady yourself, Doc," Jordan instructed.

The doctor closed his eyes, took a deep breath, and counted to three. When he opened his eyes, he managed to slide the key in with ease. "Got it."

They slipped into the nursery quietly and shut the door behind them. Doctor Monroe was on the other side of the room, hovering near Timothy's bassinet, seemingly unaware she had visitors. Popal signaled to Jordan to stay where he was before slowly walking toward the afflicted woman and child, bottle in hand. He was three-quarters of the way when Doctor Monroe noticed him. Snarling at Popal, she moved closer to Timothy.

Popal continued to advance toward her. "Hi, Lauren. I brought something." He held the bottle up for her to see. "It's time for Timothy's feeding." He was within inches of them. "You know how important it is for a baby to have its bottle. I bet he's pretty hungry right now."

He leaned over to put the bottle in Timothy's bassinet, something he'd done many times, but Doctor Monroe grabbed his arm. Jordan hurried to them, prepared to put her out of her misery.

"No, don't," Popal exclaimed. "Look at her!" Look at what she is doing."

Jordan hadn't noticed until then what Doctor Monroe was doing with her free hand. While she was holding Doctor Popal's arm with one hand, she was clumsily reaching for the bottle with the other. She continued to snarl at both of them and bit at the air a few times, but she didn't attempt to hurt them. It was almost as if she was trying to protect Timothy by warning them off but didn't want to hurt them.

"She's never done this before," Popal told him in a low, calm voice. "Usually she lets me put the bottle next to him then she picks it up. She's never grabbed me or taken the bottle from me like this. Not going to lie, kinda scared the shit out of me, but I don't think she aims to hurt me." As Doctor Monroe wrapped her fingers around the bottle, he placed his free hand over the hand she was using to hold his arm. "Lauren, I miss you. Are you still in there?"

She reacted more like a human than one of the afflicted. When she felt his touch, she appeared startled and snarled a bit louder but then she quieted down. She looked at Popal with what could be perceived as recognition in her eyes. As shocked as Doctor Popal and Jordan were by her initial reaction, they were floored when she pulled her hand from underneath his, placed it over his, and gave his hand a gentle and affectionate squeeze. It was a brief and simple action yet; it had a massive impact on Jordan and Popal.

Doctor Monroe released Popal's hand, took the bottle, and moved to Timothy. Jordan knew he shouldn't do anything that could possibly antagonize her, but he moved closer to get a better look. He couldn't help himself, he needed to see that baby up close. Doctor Monroe's hand shook and twitched, making it difficult for her to get the nipple in Timothy's mouth, but she was successful after a few tries. Jordan continued to move in until he was next to Timothy's bassinet. He looked down at the tiny afflicted happily sucking on his bottle. Jordan hadn't been sure how he would feel when he truly got a good look at the baby, but he'd thought it would be something along the lines of repulsion. He was surprised when he realized repulsion wasn't something he felt. He watched Timothy taking his bottle and took note of the little sounds he made, the way his little fingers moved, and the way he occasionally kicked his legs. They were all things happy, living babies did. If not for the boy's discolored skin and pale, almost white eyes one could easily mistake him for a living baby. No, Jordan didn't feel repulsed as he watched him. Instead, he felt sadness because the little one would never know what it was to feel human love because he would always be seen as a monster or abomination. He felt angered by the fact people had been so foolish, selfish, and cruel they'd put things in motion that led to Timothy's condition. He was an innocent, and it was the ultimate injustice that he paid the price for what others had done. Without forethought he gingerly caressed the baby's head, and Timothy cooed at the feel of his touch. He appeared to enjoy Jordan's compassionate touch, continuing to coo, wiggle, and close his eyes, but Doctor Monroe was not pleased with it. She started to snarl and gnash her teeth.

Jordan's instincts told him he should back away, but he ignored them. He continued to stroke the baby's head and made it a point to look Doctor Monroe in the eyes as he spoke to her. "Hush now. Lauren, is it? That's your name? Well, Lauren, you don't' have to get upset."

She became more agitated, gnashing her teeth more aggressively.

"Jordan, what are you doing," Popal asked, a quiver in his voice. "Step away."

Jordan never broke eye contact with Lauren. "Talk to her, Doc. She trusts you. Tell her I'm not a threat."

Popal swallowed hard. "Lauren, look at me." When she didn't respond he grabbed her hand and held it between both of his, causing her to whip her head around to look at him and growl violently. "Lauren, it's me. Look at me. You know me, and you know I wouldn't let anyone in here I thought might hurt you or Timothy. I don't know how much of you is left in there, but I know if there is anything left of you, you know I wouldn't allow that. Please, trust me, he means no harm. He's a friend."

That look of recognition returned to her eyes. She gazed into Popal's eyes then down to her hand clasped between his and instantly calmed down. When Jordan called her name, she looked at him but remained calm.

"Lauren, my name is Jordan, and Doctor Popal is telling you the truth. I will not hurt you as long as you don't hurt anyone, and I don't think you want to hurt anyone. I know

Timothy can't hurt anyone so, I won't hurt him either. In fact, this world let him down, and I hate that. I wish it hadn't happened. It's heartbreaking and wrong, but he is lucky in some ways because he has you and Doctor Popal. He has me now too, and I will protect you both. You don't have to do it alone anymore, and I promise my friends and I are going to do everything we can to help you both."

He went to the nursery window and closed the curtains, then he proceeded to lock the nursery door and start placing furniture against it.

Popal was perplexed. "What are you doing?"

"I just told her I would protect them, and I am trying to gain her trust." He hurriedly pushed a cabinet against the rest of the furniture he already had in place and rejoined Popal on the other side of the room. "If we are going to have any hope of helping her humanity to resurface and grow we have to treat her like a human being. Part of that is earning her trust and giving her trust. So, instead of going to another room, we are going to stay right here and protect them from anything coming through that door and trust she won't eat us."

Gray and Capp formulated a dual-purpose plan of attack. It would drastically reduce the risk of harm or death for their people and reduce the odds of their people catching a glimpse of the nursery's occupants. Knowing most of the afflicted from the bunker had followed JC, Hobo, and Paytan into the stairwell, they assumed there would only be a manageable few left on the first floor or in the basement and bunker. With that in mind, they instructed their people to clear those areas then position themselves outside in front of the emergency room doors. They were to open the doors as wide as possible to allow Capp and Gray to lead the afflicted outside where everyone would open fire on them. Their hope was it would be safer for all involved and alert Jordan to their presence, giving him time to hide Doctor Monroe and Timothy if he hadn't already. The group put their trust in Capp and Gray and set about the task at hand with courage and determination.

The group made quick work of the first phase of the plan then readied for the second phase by opening the emergency room doors and getting into position. Capp opened the stairwell door on the first floor as quietly as he could. To keep it open he tied one end of a phone cord to the door and the other end to the handrail behind the door in the stairwell. He looked back to the group waiting outside then to Gray who signified his readiness with a nod. The two of them slowly crept up the stairs. On the second floor landing they found three afflicted. Two were stumbling around aimlessly, but the third was lying on her stomach, her torso and head thrashing about. One of her legs was almost severed at the knee, and the other was clearly crushed as was one of her arms. Her other arm was bent backward at the elbow with a bone protruding from her forearm. It appeared she'd fallen on the way up and been trampled by the others. Capp and Gray used their knives to dispatch them without making any noise to alert the other afflicted. Continuing to advance up the stairs, they could hear the moans and grunts of the other afflicted growing louder. They didn't sound as frenzied as they had earlier, but it was clear they were restless.

Just before reaching the third floor landing, they found the tail end of the group of afflicted that chased JC, Hobo, and Paytan up to the fourth floor. They'd known there were several of them, but they hadn't realized it was such a large amount until that moment. The two men exchanged glances, each one knowing what the other was thinking and feeling without either speaking a word.

Capp silently mouthed a countdown. When he hit three, he stomped the floor and slapped the wall. "Hey, stupids!" The afflicted turned to him. "Yeah, that's right, I called y'all stupid! Got a problem with it?"

Gray tapped the handrail next to him with his knife. "Fresh meat, boys and girls! Get it while it's still normal body temp!"

The afflicted began to move toward them, and Capp grinned. "Hope you like fast food, idiots!"

"That's Capp and Gray," Jordan whispered.

Popal looked at the nursery door, terrified someone was about to burst through it. "You can't know for certain."

"Did you hear those smart-ass remarks? Trust me, it's them. I'm going to go back to the ladder and go down to help them. Maybe you should go back to the other room until I come to get you."

"I will stay here."

Jordan's face was filled with concern. His eyes darted to Lauren who was still feeding Timothy. "Just go back to the other room as a a precaution."

"You said we had to treat them as humans, and I don't hide from humans I care about. Besides, I always take precautions." He pulled up the leg of his scrubs to reveal a pistol strapped to his calf.

"Well, okay then."

Capp and Gray backed down the stairs, continually hurling insults at the afflicted and making sure to keep a healthy distance between themselves and the afflicted steadily moving toward them. It only took a couple of minutes for them to reach the first floor, but it felt like hours. They led the afflicted to the emergency room doors and rushed to join their group outside. Once Capp and Gray were safely out of the line of fire, the group unleashed on them. The first couple of waves of afflicted were mowed down easily as they came out the hospital doors, but the bodies piled up in front of the doors creating a blockage, preventing the afflicted behind them from making their way out.

Jordan, unnoticed by the others, had made it to the parking lot, and when he saw what was happening he sprang into action. Rushing to the doors, he began dragging bodies away while trying to maintain a safe distance from the afflicted trying to push and claw their way out.

Gray sprinted over to help. "We don't have to move them far, just far enough to clear a small path!"

Jordan bent to grab the arms of another body, so focused on getting a path cleared he didn't notice the body underneath it was still moving. It grasped his ankle and with a yank sent him toppling backward. Jordan landed violently on his back, knocking the wind out of him and sending his gun flying. He was too dazed to comprehend what had just happened or that his assailant had nearly freed itself from the body it was under. Seeing what was happening, Gray started toward Jordan, but before he could reach him, several of the afflicted inside managed to push through the pile of bodies. Gray knew he had to deal with them before going to Jordan otherwise, the afflicted still gripping Jordan's ankle would be the least of their problems. JC and Capp moved to help Gray, and Hobo led the rest of the group to handle the large amount of afflicted emerging from the nearby woods, apparently drawn by the commotion at the hospital. Everyone was quite literally in a fight for their lives. Everyone except for Chester.

Chester was frozen. No matter how hard he tried he couldn't make his legs move. It wasn't the first time he'd faced the afflicted, but he'd never faced that many at once. He remembered nightmares he had as a child, particularly one. In that dream he was being hunted by some unseen monster. Although he couldn't see his stalker, he could sense its dark presence. He could almost feel it breathing on his neck, and he couldn't move. Seeing the afflicted all around them, his legs felt made of lead, very much as they had in that childhood nightmare. For a brief moment, he contemplated the possibility he was still that nine-year-old boy stuck in a nightmare. He looked at the havoc surrounding him, his eyes landing on Jordan who was still dazed and struggling to kick the afflicted from his ankle and drag himself away from it.

Chester watched in horror as another afflicted advanced on Jordan until it was looming over him. Nobody at Sandbox had ever been hateful or unkind to Chester, but none of them had been as kind to him or shown as much faith in him as Hobo and Jordan had. Remembering that stirred something in him because his legs suddenly worked again. Before he had time to think about what he was doing, he sprinted to Jordan. The afflicted standing over Jordan was reaching down for him. Chester promptly plunged his knife into its ear and pushed it away from Jordan. He then grabbed the hair of the afflicted latched onto Jordan's ankle, jerked its head back with a ferocity he never knew he possessed, and pushed his knife blade into its eye. Having successfully eliminated the two most pressing threats to Jordan, Chester knew they had only a matter of seconds before more descended on them.

"Come on," Chester instructed, pulling the dead afflicted from Jordan's feet. "We gotta move! Let's go, bud!"

Jordan shook his head, not to disagree with Chester but rather in an effort to shake the cobwebs from his mind. He tried to speak, but due to the pain he was feeling and still gasping for breath, all he managed to get out was a garbled groan. Despite the pain, he managed to roll onto his side and prop himself up on his elbow. Chester retrieved Jordan's gun from the spot it had landed moments earlier. Jordan made it to his knees, and Chester gave him his gun, slid his hands under Jordan's arms from behind, and hoisted him to his feet. An afflicted grabbed Chester's shoulder. Still holding onto Jordan, Chester whirled around to face the afflicted, and Jordan landed a shot in the middle of its forehead.

Capp collapsed in an exhausted heap on the parking lot pavement outside the hospital.

Gray squatted in front of him. "You okay, man?"

Capp gazed in dismay at the scene around them. Everywhere he looked there were lifeless bodies. He was relieved none of them were anyone from Sandbox, yet he couldn't help but feel a sense of sorrow. "Look at them. Were any of them the same as Mike? Was some part of them the same as us? Even if they were neither, they were just like us once upon a time. They had jobs, homes, families." He pointed to the body of a male afflicted close to them. "Take that poor bastard. That guy probably had a girlfriend that drove him nuts, but he loved her more than his own life." He pointed to the body of a female afflicted. "And her, she looks like she was in her late teens, early twenties maybe. Bet she had a part-time job, maybe as a waitress, while she went to college. She was the apple of her daddy's eye and her mama's pride and joy." Capp looked down at his bloody, shaking hands. "I'm sorry. Sometimes it just hits me harder than others how screwed up and unfair this whole damned situation is."

Gray understood what he meant as those same types of thoughts tormented him as well. He did his best to block them out, but sometimes there was no way to keep the heart-wrenching thoughts at bay. "Capp, I get it. This is all unfair bullshit, but it is what it is. Sometimes it gnaws at me, but you want to know what gets me through it and keeps me going?"

"What's that?"

"Your daughter, Jordan, Tooter, Giga, and all the other young, innocent, and helpless ones who are still here. We suppress our heartbreak and those painful thoughts to keep going for them because they deserve to be protected, to be loved, and to have a chance at having a life. We are the only ones who can give them any of that. Whether we asked for that responsibility or not, it is ours now. They're ours, and we're their hope."

Capp raised his eyes to meet Gray's. "Most of the time I only look at it as making sure Gracie and the others survive, but I forget living is about so much more than just surviving. Thanks for giving me a little reminder."

Gray smiled at his friend. "Hey, we're family, brother. We keep each other going. It's what we do."

A few feet away JC, Hobo, and Chester were inspecting Jordan's leg.

"Are you sure you weren't bit," JC asked as Hobo raised Jordan's pant leg in search of bite marks or injuries. "Don't be afraid to tell us if you were. We won't hurt you. We could possibly amputate the affected area, which might stop the spread of the affliction, or we could quarantine you and do our best to treat you. If worse comes to worst, we will work to rehab you. We will figure out something."

"I was out of it for a hot minute, but I don't think I was bit. What about it, Hobo? Was I nibbled on?"

Hobo lowered Jordan's pant leg. "Negatory. I see no

signs that you were nibbled, but not for lack of that afflicted trying. There are obvious gnaw marks on the sole of your boot, but luckily for you, that's the extent of the damage. Well, other than some bruises and that gnarly goose egg on the back of your head. I'd be willing to bet you have a mild concussion. We should have Professor Jorgen take a look at you."

JC felt that was a wise idea. "Absolutely. Why don't you take him back to Sandbox to get that done and bring some more people back here with you to help with this cleanup."

Jordan frowned. "No! Not until I introduce you to Doctor Popal. He can check me out too."

"What's going on, guys? How's our boy," Capp asked as he and Gray joined them.

Gray addressed Jordan directly. "You look like you're okay. Glad to see that, but I'm curious as to where you came from. As far as I knew you were still on the fourth floor."

"I was. I made sure the others on the fourth floor would remain unseen and quiet then went out the window to help you all."

Chester was curious. "What did you do to keep them quiet? How did you keep an afflicted baby from making noise or crying?"

Jordan half-shrugged. "We had Lauren, uh, Doctor Monroe give Timothy a bottle."

Everyone's mouths gapped open, but before they could question him further, they saw Paytan, accompanied by a few other men, approaching.

"Just wanted to let you guys know we're gonna head in and make sure the hospital is completely clear," Paytan offered.

"No," JC, Capp, Gray, Hobo, Jordan, and Chester shouted simultaneously, startling Paytan and the other men.

"Um, okay," a bewildered Paytan stammered.

JC nervously snickered. "Sorry about that. It's just that we were about to do that ourselves. We were finalizing our plan of action."

"Yeah, we've got this covered," Capp chimed in. "You could be of more help by staying out here and organizing this cleanup. Those bodies will cause one more hell of a stink before long. Might be wise to put together a crew to make sure the town is clear and take care of any stragglers coming out of the woods too. We can't afford any surprises."

Paytan, while suspicious, sensed it was best to do as Capp instructed. "Sure thing. We're on it."

Capp stared through the nursery window. His emotions and thoughts were in a tailspin. He'd become accustomed to Mike, even marveling at his humanity and progress, but looking at Lauren and Timothy, he knew this was something different. Lauren didn't possess the verbal, social, or motor skills Mike did, but she did have the skills and compassion to care for another being, a completely helpless being. As for Timothy, he appeared to have the ability of any other infant to communicate his needs, mainly hunger, and to feel affection and love. Part of him wanted to turn away, to dismiss what he was seeing as a figment of his imagination. His mind told him what he was seeing wasn't possible. None of what was happening in the world should have been possible. The dead shouldn't rise up and walk yet, the afflicted did indeed roam the earth, and that presented a whole host of questions & uncertainties that part of him had been pondering in one way or another since Roma. That part of him was utterly fascinated by the scene unfolding before him and utterly devastated by it. It confirmed the possibility of some humanity remaining in all the afflicted he'd put down. That possibility made him feel like a murderer. Then there was Timothy, an innocent baby whose life hadn't truly begun, now condemned to be one of the afflicted. Capp felt as if that baby might break him. He hoped none of the others could see his hands trembling, his eyes tearing up, or his knees wobbling. He thought back to what Gray said to him earlier, and it helped to calm him. "We're their hope," he whispered under his breath.

"Doctor Popal, standing next to him, heard him but couldn't make out what he said. "Excuse me?"

"Uh, um, I was just stating we have to keep them hidden for their safety. They're remarkable, and they could be invaluable in the future. They offer some hope."

Popal sighed with relief. "I am so glad you see it that way. To be perfectly honest, I was afraid the lot of you would think I was crazy or kill them."

Chester cleared his throat to get their attention. "Welp, everyone who needs to be is now filled in on this little situation so, how about somebody fill me in on whatever the situation is with Mike?"

An uncomfortable silence fell over the group.

Doctor Popal waited for someone to speak, but when no

one did he took it upon himself to break the silence. "I too would be interested in hearing about this Mike as I heard him mentioned earlier."

No one spoke.

"For Christ's sake," Jordan yelled. "I'd say Doctor Popal and Chester have earned some trust! Not only that, but they could be very helpful. What choice do we really have considering everything they've already seen and heard?"

"We all know he's right," Gray pointed out.

JC exhaled loudly and sharply. "I believe he is. We should secure the nursery and find somewhere to have a very long and very honest conversation."

"That's an excellent idea. However, we would be a little safer if we cleared the surgical room full of afflicted first," Gray suggested. "Plus, wouldn't want any of the others coming across them unexpectedly. Could go sideways if they did."

Hobo, who had remained silent the entire time, was alarmed. "Wait. What? Did you say something about a surgical room full of afflicted?"

"Did we forget to mention that," Gray asked sheepishly.

Hobo turned to Jordan.

"Don't look at me," Jordan quipped. "Gray's older than me, he should have known better than to forget that. I'm just a dumb kid following my elder's lead."

Gray glared at him. "Now that you mention it, I think I did say something about them when Hobo, JC, and Paytan came busting through the stairwell door."

"Well, excuse me for not catching it," Hobo said incredulously. "It was a slightly stressful situation!"

"Can y'all handle it without me," Capp asked. "I'll stay here with Doctor Popal. We'll make sure nobody discovers our friends up here. I don't think you'll have any problems without me, after all, you've got Chester, who as it turns out, can kick some major butt."

Gray gave Chester a playful punch on the arm. "Yeah, you've been holding out on us."

Chester blushed.

Hobo beamed like a proud father. "Yep, Chester, turns out you're a total bad ass with no alcohol required. I, on the other hand, will require multiple Hobo cookies at the end of this day."

As Capp predicted, the others took care of the afflicted in the third-floor operating room without any issues while he and Popal kept guard over the nursery. Capp took the opportunity to tell Popal about himself, the rest of the group, and Sandbox. When the others returned they gathered chairs to sit near the stairwell door so as to better hear and intercept anyone who might wander up the stairs. Sitting there they explained most everything to Doctor Popal and Chester, going all the way back to Russo and R-Bug. Popal and Chester sat speechless for a while. The rest of the group sat in silence with them, allowing them time to process what they'd just been told.

Chester spoke first. "So, uh, you're telling me Mike is like that doctor and baby in there? Oh, and he is at Sandbox, and you were keeping it a secret from everyone? That about cover it?"

JC nodded in the affirmative.

Popal stood and began to pace. "That is certainly some story. You've all been through so much. The fact you've survived and been willing to keep open minds while taking a scientific approach to things... It's admirable and incredible. If you would allow me, I would very much like to join your efforts, to meet your Mike, and to have Lauren and Timothy join your research. Perhaps they could learn from Mike and vice versa. We could be embarking on an exciting, interesting, and important journey together."

Chester impulsively slapped his knee and stomped his foot before getting up from his chair and storming off.

Jordan rose to follow him. "I got him."

Hobo trailed after Jordan. "I'm coming with you."

JC watched them leave before turning his attention back to Doctor Popal. "I'm happy you feel that way, Doctor. I would like to propose we do all those things and more. I would like to have you as a citizen of Sandbox, and if you're willing, I would like you to not only join our research team but also be our main medical provider. Professor Jorgen does have some medical training, but he prefers the research side of things. I would also very much like to make this town, this hospital, and the facility below into an extension of Sandbox. Maybe we should even consider connecting The Underneath to your underground facility and move Mike, Doctor Monro, and Timothy into some type of homey environment down there."

Doctor Popal extended his hand to JC. "I'm all in."

"Chester, hold up," Jordan pleaded.

Chester stopped, allowing both Jordan and Hobo to catch up to him. "You know something," he bellowed as he turned to face them, "I'm not upset about Mike, well, I'm not happy he was turned, it's a tragedy, but I'm fine with him being there and you all trying to help him. What bothers me is it being kept from the rest of us. If, God forbid, something had gone wrong, if he had turned full afflicted and escaped, none of us would have been prepared to protect ourselves or the children because we had no clue there was a possible threat living with us. Do you not see how unbelievably screwed up that is?"

"Chester, you have every right to be mad, but you have to see the position we were in," Hobo reasoned. "We didn't like keeping it from any of you. I can't stress enough how much we disliked it, but our fear was if we told you one of two things would happen. Number one, it would create a panic, and in a panic, people would get sloppy, they'd be irrational, and they'd run on fear. Those circumstances could and likely would result in behavior and mistakes that would cause the deaths of people we love. Number two, someone would put Mike down out of fear, and by doing so they'd kill someone who is at least partially still human and one of us. Any hope of discovering a cure would almost certainly die along with him. We were in a horrible position and had to do what we felt was best for everyone at Sandbox, for Mike, and for humanity overall."

"Man, Chester, I get it," Jordan told him. "This whole thing sucks. The world sucks as a whole at this point. That is why keeping Sandbox and Mike safe is so important. Mike may hold the key to a cure, and if that falls through then communities like Sandbox will be the key to rebuilding the world. Hell, we might even be able to rebuild it better than it was before. Either way, whether through Mike or through Sandbox, we have a chance to take the suck out of the world. All of that was what we had on our minds when we were put in a position none of us could have ever imagined."

Chester walked over to the nursery window and watched for a moment as Lauren gingerly touched Timothy's tiny arm. The infant wiggled and made a noise closely resembling the coo a normal baby would make when it was content or happy. As angry as Chester was, he couldn't deny the afflicted woman and child were proof the possibility the afflicted had humanity left in them was more likely than not. If Mike truly was like them, he could understand why JC and the others made the choices they'd made. "So, Mike's like them?"

"Yes," Hobo answered. "In some ways he is more advanced than they are. He can even speak."

Upon hearing that Chester knew what he had to do. He spun on his heels and practically charged back to JC. Hobo and Jordan were right on his heels.

Chester marched up to JC like a man on a mission. "I still believe keeping Mike at Sandbox without telling us was wrong and reckless!"

"JC didn't make that decision alone," Capp informed him. Several of us were involved in making that decision. You can't place all the blame on his shoulders."

JC held up his hand to silence Capp. "Others did weigh in on the matter, but ultimately the final decision was mine, as are the repercussions of that decision. Chester is entitled to his anger and to express it."

Chester calmed down some, but his tone remained firm. "I am mad, but I understand why you did it. Mike, Doctor Monroe, and Timothy could be the answer to many people's prayers. After watching Doctor Monroe and Timothy, even if they can't help us develop a vaccine or cure, there is no denying some part of them is still human. Perhaps they and others like them are sick or afflicted as you say. I have no qualms about putting down the ones who seem to have no humanity at all, but I'm conflicted when it comes to Mike, Doctor Monroe, and Timothy. In some ways I think the most merciful thing that could be done for them is to put them down, but I honestly don't think I could. Not because they represent hope for a cure but because... How can I put this? Put it this way, we don't simply put down cancer patients. No, we show them compassion, we try to save them, and if we can't save them, well, in those cases we try to make them comfortable and show them kindness. Mike and Doctor Monroe were good people who did a lot of good in this world. Timothy is as innocent as they come. None of them deserved the hand they were dealt, but they do deserve a chance and compassion. I will keep your secret, and I will help protect them."

It was then JC made a statement that stunned them all. "While I appreciate your understanding and your willingness to keep what you know under your hat, there will be no more secrets. Sandbox is full of people such as yourself. They're good people with the ability to put their fear aside in order to think critically and objectively. We should have trusted them, and we will start doing so right now. Hopefully they understand, and if we're lucky, they will contribute to our mission and research with each of their unique talents and skills. And in the spirit of being honest and trusting, there is another secret. It's about someone I would like to bring to Sandbox."

"Is this person like Lauren and Timothy," Popal inquired.

"No, she is a very unique child. She is Hope."

Gray leaned forward in his chair. "While we were with Kickz and his group we came across a young couple, and the girl was pregnant. Long story short, they were mixed up with some bad people, and the next time we saw them, they'd been executed and turned. JC managed to save the unborn baby. He delivered her by cesarean, and she was healthy and normal. He named her Hope. When we left the group in Florida, we decided it was probably safer for her to leave her in their care."

Doctor Popal had been excited when he learned about Mike, but upon hearing about Hope he became positively giddy. "And you plan to bring this baby here?"

JC nodded. "Perhaps. I will reserve the final decision on that until we've had a chance to gauge everyone's reactions to the multiple bombs we are about to drop on them."

"Probably a good idea," Capp acknowledged.

"Hobo," JC began, "of those who are currently outside please, choose those you feel will be most receptive to everything we have to tell them. Gather those chosen in the hospital cafeteria and send everyone else back to

Sandbox. I feel we may have a better chance of making this work if we ease into it. We will tell everything to the people Hobo chooses, then enlist them to help us tell the others."

Hobo went down to the parking lot to select those who would go to the cafeteria. He believed most everyone present would get over the inevitable and understandable shock they would feel, but he was careful to pick those who would not only recover from it the quickest but were also held in high regard by the others. In the end, nine were chosen and escorted to the cafeteria where JC and the others joined them. Just as he had done with Doctor Popal and Chester, JC told them about everything, including Mike, Hope, Lauren, and little Timothy. He apologized for having kept things from them and let them know it was okay if they were angry but asked them to allow him the chance to explain what he hoped to accomplish in the way of a vaccine or cure and with the small town they'd just cleared. They granted his request, listening in earnest as he explained how the humanity in Mike, Lauren, and Timothy not only made them different from the other afflicted but also provided hope for a cure or possible rehabilitation for the afflicted and how baby Hope's blood could contain antibodies. They continued to listen as he explained his desire to make the small town an extension of Sandbox, making both places along with Kickz's settlement in Florida key players in rebuilding the United States and eventually the world, whether a cure was developed or not.

"In short," JC continued, "the world and society we once knew are no longer and never will be again. It is a sad fact in many ways, but in others, it is an opportunity. It is an opportunity for us to rebuild better, to avoid the mistakes of the past. Between everyone at Sandbox and the Florida settlement, we have some of the finest minds and most courageous souls to ever grace this planet. That alone ensures we will succeed."

Capp stood to address the room. "What he is saying is each and every person in this hospital, back at Sandbox, and in Florida are the most badass of the badasses in one way or another. As such, whether or not this is mankind's extinction event is entirely on our shoulders. So, what will it be? Will we put trust in each other and work together, or will we allow ourselves to become extinct?"

Lawrence was the first to respond. "Before I commit to anything, I'd like to see the bunker facility, Doctor Monroe, and Timothy. I imagine we all would."

JC readily agreed, choosing to have Doctor Popal show them the underground facility first. JC hadn't had an opportunity to see it himself and was looking forward to it. The bunker did not disappoint. When JC designed and built The Underneath, he'd done his very best to ensure it was a top-of-the-line facility, but he hadn't had the funds or resources the company that built the bunker had. The bunker facility was truly state-of-the-art, and JC felt like a kid at Disney World. He was positive Professor Jorgen would feel the same, and although Lawrence, a chemist, wasn't saying much, JC could see he was in awe of it as well.

After the tour of the bunker everyone went to the nursery on the fourth floor. Lawrence and the other eight people Hobo had chosen gazed through the nursery window in dumbfounded disbelief. Timothy was fussy and Doctor Monro was attempting to comfort him by stroking his head.

Lawrence turned to face JC. "I won't deny this is unusual, even somewhat impressive, but it could be just some echo of a deeply buried, basic instinct."

Capp stepped in to address Lawrence's concern before JC could. "I can see how that hypothesis could be correct, however, there is evidence to the contrary. Mike can speak, and he is capable of doing some basic writing and coloring. He's been making steady progress."

"I've been in a room with Doctor Monroe as well as Mike," Jordan informed Lawrence. "Neither of them hurt me, and I can promise you, it is more than an echo. They can understand us, and they have feelings."

Gray was stunned by Jordan's revelation. "Hold on! You went in there with her?"

"Yeah, I did, but I'll tell you about it later. Right now the point is Doctor Popal and I were able to safely communicate with her. She showed caring for Doctor Popal and Timothy and showed understanding for what I said to her."

Doctor Popal suddenly had an idea. "Hold that thought!" He darted away from them, disappearing down the hall, but returned quickly, holding up a bottle ready for Timothy. "Maybe this will be enough proof for all of you. Jordan, shall we?"

"Yup. Let's do it."

Popal and Jordan slipped into the nursery.

"Lauren," Popal called softly. "Lauren, it's time for Timothy's feeding." He held up the bottle for her to see.

The men walked slowly to Timothy's bassinet. Lauren calmly looked at Popal but became agitated when she looked at Jordan.

"Miss Lauren, why you gotta be that way," Jordan asked. "Didn't we have this talk earlier? Try to remember now. I came in with the doc and we talked. I told you I would protect you and Timothy. Do you remember?" He looked at Timothy then back to her. "Here, maybe this will help you remember." Very cautiously he reached for Timothy. "See," he said as he gently rubbed Timothy's head. "Remember this?"

Everyone watching from the window collectively held their breath. Most of them were certain Lauren was going to attack Jordan and force him to put her down.

Doctor Popal spoke gently to Lauren. "Doctor Monroe, Jordan and his friends are here to help. They're our friends. See them in the window?"

Lauren took a few steps back when she saw everyone staring at her, and she made a sound that almost sounded like a whimper. For a moment she appeared to be frightened.

Jordan kept his eyes on Lauren while reaching to take the bottle from Popal. "Don't be scared Miss Lauren. They're friends, and I swear they won't hurt you. We all just want to help. See, watch." He softly ran the tip of the bottle nipple across Timothy's lips to get his attention. Timothy quickly latched on. "Well, look at that Miss Lauren. He trusts me, and I know I'm not as good at this as you are, but I'm learning. Like I said before, you don't have to do it alone anymore."

Lauren twisted her neck and tilted her head as she watched Jordan feed Timothy and stroke his tiny head. She took a few shaky steps forward until she was close enough to reach the hand Jordan was using to feed Timothy. Jordan remained calm and steady when she placed her hand over his to adjust the angle he had the bottle tilted at.

"Was I holding it wrong? I'm new to feeding babies, hell, new to pretty much everything with babies. So, I'm going to need you to teach me. Is that okay?"

Lauren nodded.

"Thank you, Miss Lauren. I have a feeling we're all going to learn a lot about babies and love from you. Right now Doctor Popal and I need to step out there to talk to our friends. While we do that, can you finish feeding Timothy?" Jordan slipped his hand from under hers, and she immediately gripped the bottle and kept it steady, ensuring Timothy wasn't disrupted. "There ya go, Miss Lauren. Timothy is so lucky to have you, and I am so happy to know you."

Popal gingerly placed a hand on her shoulder. "Lauren, I'll bring your dinner soon."

Using her free hand, she patted his hand and gave it a gentle squeeze. Popal felt a lump in his throat as he returned her squeeze before exiting the room with Jordan.

"I...I..." Lawrence stammered. "I've never seen anything like it. She showed emotions, she didn't attack you and she is feeding the baby! She even corrected the way you were feeding him! This changes everything."

Doctor Popal stared at Doctor Monroe lovingly. "She's always been a remarkable woman, first in life and now in death."

Clara, Bobby's wife, and a retired NASA employee wiped a tear from her cheek. "That is obvious, and right now she is a shining example of the strength of the human spirit."

"Does that mean you're with us," Capp asked.

Clara, never looking away from nursery window, answered, "Damn straight I am."

"As am I," Lawrence interjected.

With that, the remaining seven of the chosen group echoed Clara's and Lawrence's sentiments in their own ways.

JC's delight was written all over his face. "This is excellent news! Now we, as a group, need to decide how to proceed with the others at home in Sandbox."

During the discussion that followed multiple decisions were made. Naturally, the main topic of the discussion was regarding how to get everyone at Sandbox on board. They debated on again picking a small handful of people to fill in and then enlisting their help in convincing the others but thought better of it for fear it could be perceived as an underhanded manipulation. In the end it was decided it would be best to gather everyone together, tell them all at once, and hope they'd be as open-minded as Hobo's chosen nine had been. Because of the strenuous and exhausting events of the day as well as it being late in the day, they thought it was best to wait until the next morning to gather everyone and to postpone the scouting mission to the asylum for a day or two. Capp and Jordan volunteered to spend the night at the hospital to stand watch over Doctor Popal, Doctor Monroe, Timothy, and of course, the cat.

Alice was sitting at a picnic table eating a bowl of the vegetable soup Bobby had made when she saw Bobby's wife, Clara, arrive with Hobo, JC, and a man she didn't recognize. Her last encounter with JC had been a bit odd to say the least, but she still wanted to properly introduce herself to him seeing as he was one of the founders of Sandbox. JC was helping himself to a bowl of soup and chatting with Clara when Alice approached them.

"Hello, JC. We haven't properly met. I'm Alice, and it's very nice to meet you."

JC looked at her strangely but did shake her outstretched hand. "Uh, yeah. Hi, but I thought we met when you showed up unannounced the other day."

Clara gave JC a light slap on the arm. "Mind your manners, Mister! Alice, you'll have to excuse JC. He's somewhat dense when it comes to socializing and manners. JC, Alice came to us after the outbreak, and she has truly become one of us."

"That's, um, nice, I guess."

Clara ignored JC's less than warming response and motioned to the man Alice hadn't recognized. "Alice, this young man is Gray."

Gray gave Alice a nod. "Pleased to meet you."

"You too. Gray is an unusual name though."

"It's kind of a nickname."

"I see. Well, I was enjoying a bowl of Bobby's soup. I hate eating alone. Would you all like to join me?"

"Of course we would, sweetie," Clara answered before JC could object.

Once they were seated at Alice's table JC, despite feeling Alice's need to meet him was odd, decided it might be a good idea to learn a little about her, especially considering she would be at the village meeting the following morning. He hoped he could get an idea of whether or not she would be an ally. "Alice, how did you come to be here at Sandbox?"

"A few days before the outbreak I'd come to Virginia to interview for a job and look at some houses. My kids are grown, but we've been through a lot these past few years, and I thought a fresh start would be good for us. I was in Richmond when the outbreak started. The kids had gone to a con or something in Arizona, and I kept trying to call them, but they never answered. RIC had been shut down, no flights in or out so, I decided to drive to Arizona. I knew it wasn't logical, but to be frank, I didn't give a damn about logic. All I cared about was finding my kids."

Gray recognized her story. "Hobo told me about you. The doctor found you and brought you here."

"She did. As you can imagine, getting out of Richmond was no easy task during the beginning of the outbreak. Traffic was backed up for miles on every road out of the city. Then the zombies started showing up. I abandoned my car and tried to make it out on foot. Honestly, I was surprised when I managed to make it to an area just a few miles from here, but then I ran into a herd of zeds in the woods. I managed to take a few of them out, but there were just too many. I was running from them when the most cliché thing happened, I fell. Classic horror movie, right? I fell and slid down a muddy hill. It was one of those good news/bad news things. The good news was that little tumble put enough space between me and them that I had time to slip away. Bad news was it also did a number on my leg. By some miracle, I made it to the highway and holed up in a car with a dead battery. I was there for two days before the doctor found me. My leg and some cuts were infected, I was burning up with fever, dehydrated, and delirious. If she hadn't brought me here, I'd be walking with the dead now. I had planned to continue to Arizona after I healed, but then I heard it was completely overrun. It wasn't long after that the doctor died. So, while I am no doctor, I do try to carry on her work by searching for survivors."

"And caring for Maria," Gray added.

Alice smiled. "Yes, then there is little Maria, my tiny savior. Effing walkers, Zs, zeds, zombies, or whatever the hell you want to call them took everything from me and that little girl, but at least we were lucky enough to find each other."

JC couldn't help but notice some of the terms she used for the afflicted. "Walkers and Zs, I take it you were a Walking Dead fan. Possibly a Z Nation fan as well."

"Guilty as charged," Alice giggled. "The Walking Dead, Fear the Walking Dead, Z Nation, and all things Romero. Basically, all things zombie really. I blame my dad. I was a kid when VCRs first came out, and I remember the day we got our first one like it was yesterday."

JC was intrigued. "How does your father and a VCR

equate to a love for zombies?"

"Daddy was so excited when we got our first one, he took me and my brother to the store and told us to pick out a VHS each. I can't remember what my brother picked out, but I clearly remember seeing the cover of the nineteen sixty-eight Night of the Living Dead. I picked it up, read the description on the back, and knew it was the one I wanted. Mama did her best to discourage Daddy from buying it, but Daddy knew I loved horror movies and had always been able to handle them, even at that young age. He bought it for me, and it ended up being the only movie that scared me. Scared the hell out of me, but it also ignited my love for the zombie genre in all forms; movies, comics, books, shows, even games. Never imagined in a million years I'd be living in a real-life version of 7 Days to Die."

JC and Gray perked up at the mention of 7 Days to Die. They exchanged knowing glances and smiles.

"A zombie fan and a gamer," Gray asked. "How do you normally fare on horde night?"

"Wait, you guys know 7 Days? It's one of my favorite games. My oldest son and I have built some phenomenal horde bases together."

They spent a few hours chatting and getting to know each other. Alice was thrilled to learn JC and Gray had made videos on 7 Days to Die, and while Clara had never been a gamer and didn't understand most of what they were talking about, seeing their enthusiasm on the subject made her wish she had given gaming a try. As they talked, Gray realized there was something about the way Alice spoke and her features that reminded him of someone, but he couldn't put his finger on who.

JC found himself liking Alice more and more the longer they talked. He decided to use the topic of zombie shows and movies to get more of a feel for how she might react to Mike. "You know, two of my favorite characters in the wide world of zombies were Bub from *Day of the Dead* and Murphy from *Z Nation*. Several people have told me I was weird for that."

Alice shook her head. "I don't think so. I always loved them myself. At their essence they were complex characters. They represented both the good in humans and the monsters in them. They personified the constant internal struggle we all deal with, you know, the whole good versus evil thing. Some of us struggle with that more than others and perhaps more on a serious scale, but we all experience it. Bub and Murphy also simultaneously represented fear and hope. They were both monsters and heroes. We could use some of that hope they represented, but so far, I haven't seen any Bubs or Murphys out there."

Gray, taking the cue from JC, decided to feel her out with a question of his own. "I always rooted for both of them, despite Murphy's many flaws, but I could see why so many people thought they should have been put down. Is the danger they present worth the risk for a little hope that may or may not pan out?"

"It has to be. Without hope what's the point of living? Without hope we might as well be zombies. Anyway, it was as plain as the nose on your face they were still human, at least in some ways. In my opinion, killing them would have been murder. Luckily, our zombies haven't put us in that moral dilemma."

JC shrugged. "You never know when things could change."

"You're not saying that you think there could be a Bub or a Murphy out there, are you," a dumbfounded Alice asked.

"Clara, Gray, what do you think? Should we?"

Gray answered first. "I think we should."

"I know we should," Clara answered. "She's a good person, and based on this conversation, I'm certain she can handle it. She could be a valuable ally tomorrow."

JC turned his attention back to Alice. "Come with us."

Capp and Jordan were making another sweep of the outside of the hospital when Jordan voiced a concern Capp hadn't been able to stop thinking about himself.

"The people at the asylum must be planning something. They know about us, there's no way they don't know about us. Why haven't they made a move? I wish they'd just do it already. This whole cat and mouse crap is worse than a full attack."

"My guess is they're probably doing exactly what we're planning to do to them, gather info and watch. As for a full attack, I want to ask you something. I realize a lot of people see you as a kid, maybe even treat you like one, but I see you. Age wise, yeah, compared to most of us, you're still kind of a kid, but that's the only sense in which you're still a kid. You're tough, you got heart, and you're no fool.

So, tell me, do you think we're ready to take on that group? Those of us who have been out in the world since the afflicted rose are ready, pretty sure we are anyway. What about the ones who have been behind the walls of Sandbox through most if not all of the outbreak? Do you think they're prepared?"

"No, I don't," Jordan answered bluntly. "Sure, they handled the afflicted here tonight pretty well, but there's a big difference between dealing with mostly slow afflicted that don't think and a large group of strategizing humans who have been hunting and killing together with military efficiency."

"You believe Trina and Paytan then?"

"I do. I just don't sense any deception from them. I suppose they could have been lying so they could get to Sandbox. Hell, I couldn't blame them if they did. A lot of people would do that to be somewhere safe with food and water. I don't believe that's what they did though. Plus, Doctor Popal said something about seeing some men in trucks, seemed like they freaked him out. To be straight with you, I'm not sure why any of us were so quick to jump to the decisions we did concerning the asylum. We should have thought it through better. I know I said I wished they'd just get a full attack over with, but that was just my frustration talking. I know even a simple recon mission should be planned better than what we did."

"You're right. I think we were all in such a hurry to address the threat we didn't slow down long enough to use logic. I am particularly disappointed in myself for that. Considering my training, I should have known better. It was a mistake I never should have made."

"Capp, when you were in the military they trained you

for a lot of things, but I'd just about bet zombie apocalypse with a dash of crazy, evil survivors wasn't one of them."

Capp laughed in spite of himself. "You're correct, but even so, most of the training they did give me would apply in apocalypse situations too. So, still a mistake I shouldn't have made. I appreciate what you're trying to do though."

"Don't go gettin' all mushy on me. Let's head back inside and lock this place down for the night."

Alice stood perfectly still, her mouth gaping open. She was at a total loss for words, and her body would not move. She tried in vain to force her mind to accept what she was seeing, but it refused to process it. Instead, it opted to have her consider any and all scenarios that might explain away what she was seeing. She considered the possibility it was an elaborate prank. She didn't truly know JC and Gray, maybe they had a warped sense of humor. She felt she did know Clara though and couldn't imagine her going along with a prank like that. She then considered the possibility it was all just a dream. She hadn't slept well for weeks, resulting in extreme fatigue which could cause hallucinations or strange dreams once she did sleep. That thought seemed to release at least part of her body from its paralysis, enabling her to pinch her left arm with her right hand. She felt it but just barely. She pinched harder and winced. She clearly felt the second pinch, so it wasn't a dream. The final scenario she considered was the possibility she was dead. Maybe she hadn't survived that first day in the woods. Maybe the doctor hadn't found her at all. Who knew what went on in the brain once they had turned? Maybe some mutation in the newly zombified brain conjured strange images and false memories of a life or time that never existed at all.

Clara moved closer to Alice. “Now, sweetie, I understand what a shock to the system this is. I only just learned about Mike and the others, and this is my first time seeing Mike, but we need you to understand some things. Well, a lot of things actually.”

JC walked over to Mike, who was sitting at a table in the living room of his home playing checkers with Professor Jorgen. “Mike, I brought some pretty women to visit you.”

Mike looked up from his game and smiled at the sight of his cousin. He then stood and made his way over to Clara and Alice, offering them a handshake. Alice’s mind told her to run, but she looked to Gray instead. Gray assured her it was okay. Trembling slightly, Alice shook Mike’s hand, and Mike managed to utter a garbled hello.

Alice, still gripping Mike’s hand, became excited. “Oh my God! He just spoke! He spoke!”

Clara watched in awe. “Well, I’ll be.”

JC held up a deck of cards. “How about a little poker while we bring Alice up to speed? Clara, fetch Bobby. He needs to hear this too, and he’s got a great poker face.”

Capp opened the door just enough to look in on Doctor Popal sleeping soundly. The cat, curled next to Popal’s legs, raised its head and flicked its tail. Capp quietly closed the door and went in search of Jordan. He found him outside the nursery where he'd placed a table and chair near the door. He was engrossed in something he was writing in a notebook.

"Getting ready for a quiz on the apocalypse," Capp teased. "I'll just go ahead and tell ya, all answers are z."

Jordan chuckled. "Dude, the dad jokes are corny. I'll give you credit though, that one was decent."

"Speaking of dads, I've never heard you mention yours. I know you were looking for your mom. Was he with her?"

"No way. God only knows where he is. Hadn't seen him in years before the apocalypse. Gray's been more of a dad to me than that jerk ever was. I never needed him anyway."

"I've watched you mature so much since we found you back in the beginning. I can't tell you how many times I've watched you and wondered if my son would have been like you. For what it's worth, your dad really missed out because I would have been thrilled if my son had been like you."

Jordan stared down at his notebook, determined to prevent Capp from seeing his watery eyes. "What'd I say about that mushy crap? None of that mess, man. None of it."

"Alright, alright. So, you going to tell me what you're working on? Is it your debut novel or something?"

"This isn't. This is a list of ideas I had for this town and for Sandbox. I drew up some fortification plans too. Was gonna run them by all of you to get your opinions."

"I'd be glad to hear about them. I'm sure the others

would be too, but let's rewind for just a minute. What did you mean a minute ago? You said, "this isn't". See in my mind, that means you do have a novel you're working on somewhere, just maybe not here."

"I might have a few things I've been working on."

Capp drug a chair over to the table to sit opposite of Jordan. "Do tell."

"My mom was... My mom is a writer. I guess I get it from her. I've been working on a kids' series since I was about twelve, and since the world ended, I've been writing about that too. I figure one day, after the world is rebuilt, they'll teach kids about all of this in school, and they'll need documentation to be able to teach it properly."

"You're writing the future history books."

"It's more than that for me. I want people to know about you, JC, Gray, and all the others. I want them to know what all of you did to save people and to rebuild."

"You mean what we did," Capp corrected. He looked at Doctor Monroe standing over Timothy. "Do you believe things may go back to normal eventually?"

"Probably not the normal we used to know but a new normal. A normal better than the way things are right now." He pointed to Doctor Monroe and Timothy. "For me, they are proof of that."

"I keep trying to figure out what they are. They're not human, but they're not like the afflicted. We've seen they have emotions so, we know they feel things that way, but what about physically? Do they feel pain? If someone gave them a neck rub, would it feel good to them? What are they?"

"Timothy does respond to being touched, and his

response proves he feels comfort from physical touch. Ultimately, it will be up to you, the professor, JC, and Doctor Popal to determine if I'm right about that and exactly what all they do feel physically, but I know you're right about their emotions because I've seen you look at Gracie the same way Doctor Monroe looks at Timothy."

That statement made Capp look closer at Doctor Monroe, and he saw Jordan was right. Doctor Monroe looked at Timothy with the same love and adoration he looked at his daughter with. Her love for Timothy was so great she focused on nothing but him, even to the exclusion of her own well-being. Her existence revolved around caring for him and protecting him "She loves him."

"Without a doubt. Exactly what they are isn't as clear though. For all we know, we could be looking at the next evolutionary step for mankind or maybe an entirely new species of human. Who knows? For now, I'm just going to think of them as a meld. Maybe they're a meld between human and afflicted, maybe they're not, but for now, that's how I'm going to look at them." Jordan pulled his eyes away from Doctor Monroe. "By the way, what's Doctor Popal doing? He'd probably be useful in this conversation."

"Sleeping like a baby."

"Having us to keep watch over them for the night is probably a load off his shoulders. Bet it's the best sleep he's gotten in a long time. Is Romero with him?"

"Who?"

"The cat. That's his name. We decided earlier."

Capp shook his head in amusement. "How do you know it's a boy?"

"Dude, if you don't know how to tell the difference, how do you even have a daughter? We checked it for berries, and sure enough, there they were. Fuzzy, little berries."

Alice bit the nail on her index finger and paced the floor. "Seriously, people? After everything you just told me, after what I've seen, you can sit around all nonchalantly playing cards!"

Everyone, including Mike, answered in unison. "Yes."

JC continued to deal the cards. "Are you going to sit back down and continue the game or not? Should I deal you in this hand?"

Bobby gathered his cards. "Yes, please, come sit, young lady. I understand what you must be feeling, but you have to realize this is one of those situations where it simply is what it is. You can't really do anything about it on your own. A majority decision will be made at the village meeting tomorrow. Until then, you may as well enjoy a friendly game. That and a cold beer should help take the edge off."

Alice stopped pacing. "Wait, you have beer?"

As if on cue, Professor Jorgen entered the room with the dog Trina and Patyan rescued by his side and an armful of bottled beer. "Did I hear somebody say they needed a beer?" He placed a beer in Alice's hand before distributing the rest to the others at the table.

"It's actually my inaugural batch," Bobby informed Alice. "If it tastes like drain pour, I apologize."

Gray took a long drink from his bottle. "No worries there,

Bobby," he said when he was done. "You've concocted yourself a mighty fine brew."

JC nodded emphatically. "Hear, hear!"

"I concur," Professor Jorgen added. "I've never tasted any finer."

Alice took her seat at the table and turned her bottle up. Her eyes fluttered and her body relaxed. "Oh, my God! That is so good!"

Bobby smiled at her over his cards. "Told ya it would take the edge off."

The dog trotted over to Alice, placing its head in her lap. "Hi there, pup." She started stroking the animal's back and realized it was missing a hind leg. "Is this the dog from the crate you told me about?"

"That would be her," Jorgen answered. "I had to amputate the leg to save her. She is healing and adapting quite quickly. She stood up within minutes of waking from the surgery. When I went to retrieve the beer, I stopped by the lab to check on her and thought it might do her good to spend time with people who aren't abusive, murderous monsters. I would think, after what she's been through, she'd find it difficult to trust people, but she appears to be at ease with you, Alice. I do hope young Jordan isn't too upset I couldn't save her leg. He had done an excellent job treating her considering the supplies he had to work with. I'm certain his and Trina's actions were what saved that little one's life."

Alice's mood seemed to shift, to become sullen. "I look forward to meeting this Jordan of yours. He sounds like a remarkable young man, and he shares the name of another remarkable young man I knew once." A single tear rolled down her cheek. She quickly wiped it away, cleared her throat, and put on a smile. "I'm sure Jordan will see you did everything you could for her, Professor."

Jorgen looked at the dog snuggling ever closer against Alice's leg. "As I've already pointed out, she seems to be at ease with you. She obviously feels safe with you. I hate leaving her alone in the lab, but when I'm watching over Mike alone or working with him, I need to be able to focus exclusively on him. Perhaps you could take her to spend time with you and Maria at those times. I think it would be good for her."

"Of course! Maria would love it. So would I for that matter. Does she have a name?"

"I've been calling her Pup because I was unsure if anyone had given her a name. Gray, do you know if anyone has? Maybe Trina and Paytan?"

"I don't believe so. I think I heard Trina say they were waiting to see more of her personality once she was feeling better."

Clara stretched in her seat. "I'd say the fact that she survived and is walking shows plenty about her personality. She's a survivor. She's tough but still has love to give."

Gray nodded to Alice. "Go ahead, give her a name befitting those traits."

"Me? Are you sure?"

Mike, sliding a card around the table with his index finger, looked at Alice and mumbled, "You, you name."

Alice flashed him a sweet smile. "I'm so in awe of you!" She looked down at the dog, "In that case, sweet pup, I christen thee Warren."

Clara, Bobby, and Jorgen were confused, but JC and Gray instantly knew where the name came from.

"I don't think I've ever heard of a girl named Warren," Clara commented.

"*Z Nation*," JC and Gray exclaimed together.

A smile swept across Mike's lips. He held up his shaky hands and managed to trace the silhouette of a woman's curves in the air. "Roberta."

Alice squealed. "Yes! Oh, Mike, you and I are going to be good friends!"

"I take it you are cool with everything you've learned tonight then. Is that correct," JC asked.

Alice looked at the dog. "What do you say, Warren? Are we cool with it?" She leaned in closer to the dog as if she was listening to its reply. "What's that? You're cool with it if I'm cool with it? I guess it's all cool then."

Bobby grinned. "Cool is excellent."

Alice sighed as she rose from her seat, explaining while she'd found the evening to be interesting and exhilarating, she had to bid them all good night because she had to pick Maria up from the movie night the school had. Gray told her he needed to pick Gracie up from the movie night too because he'd promised Capp he'd keep an eye on her for the night.

"Tooter's there too," he added. "He's either with Gracie or Maria."

Alice was surprised. "So, you're the nice man who has made Maria feel like such a big girl with the dog sitting. I didn't know Tooter was yours."

"I'm not sure if he's mine or I'm his. Since we're going

the same way, would you allow me to walk you over?"

"A gentleman in the apocalypse, a rare breed. Yes, I believe Warren and I would like that."

The night had cooled considerably. Alice drew her sweater tighter around her to guard against the chill in the air as she walked alongside Gray. "I've been here for a while now, but it never ceases to amaze me how normal it feels inside these walls. In here it's almost like the zombies, or afflicted as you say, never happened at all."

Gray looked at the lights, homes, and people around them. "It really is. This place, the settlement in Florida, Mike, Doctor Monroe, Timothy, and Hope are just the beginning of making the whole world feel like the afflicted never happened. That's why it's so important we have as many people as possible backing us on all of this."

"I get that. That's why I'm all in. I'm fully aware of the uniquely special opportunities we have here. This could be the beginning of not only a cure but an entirely new world, maybe even a chance to fix the mistakes of the old world. I feel extremely lucky to be here for it."

"We're glad you're here." He noticed Warren wasn't between them anymore. Glancing back, he saw she'd fallen behind. "Looks like this walk may be a little much for her. She's recovering well, but her body is going through a lot." He picked Warren up. "Come on, gorgeous, let me give you a lift."

"She's not a small dog. Are you sure you want to carry her? I could go get a cart to put her in."

"No, she's fine. Hey, why did you pick Warren for her?"

"Why wouldn't I? Roberta Warren is beautiful, strong, loving, and badass. This doggo has proven herself to be all of those. Warren was only fitting for her."

"I like that reasoning."

"You said your Jordan had siblings with him when you found him. Where are they now?"

"They're at the settlement in Florida. They're just as great as he is. They're all great kids."

"Why is he here instead of with them?"

"He's kind of on a personal mission of sorts. I'm glad he's here. I never had kids of my own, and I guess I've kind of adopted him. He's proven how strong he is and become an invaluable part of what we're hoping to achieve. When we found him, he was still very childlike in many ways. He was so sensitive and had such a big heart. I was afraid the world we live in now would either crush him or harden him, and I didn't want either of those to happen. Fortunately, he's gotten stronger but managed to hang on to that sensitivity and that big heart. I do think he is struggling with balancing the way we have to live now and being strong with being sensitive and having a big heart, but I know he'll figure it out."

"He's lucky to have you, and you'll help him figure it out."

"I'm the lucky one, lucky to have him and Tooter. I've never told anyone this, and I'm not sure why I feel the need to tell you, but there's been times when I wasn't sure I wanted to keep going, times I wanted to give up. Jordan and Tooter kept me going."

Alice chuckled softly. "Lord, I know that feeling all

too well. After I accepted my kids were gone, I wanted to die. I even contemplated all the ways I could do it. Let's see, first there was one of the most common, eating the barrel of my gun, but I knew they needed all the ammo they could get around here and decided against using any of it for my own selfish reasons. I considered poisoning myself, overdosing, or even cutting my wrists or throat, but I ruled all of those out because I didn't want to turn and possibly hurt someone. I had just about settled on leaving here, finding a herd of afflicted, and simply walking right into the middle of them, but Maria came along. I call her my little savior because that's exactly what she is. She was so alone, hurt, and scared. All I wanted was to help her heal and keep her safe. I thought I was helping her, but that wasn't the case at all. She was saving me. She gave me a will and a reason to live."

"I'd be willing to bet it went both ways."

"I hope so."

They were so preoccupied with their conversation they didn't notice they'd reached the school until Maria ran up to them.

"Alice! Alice, can Gracie spend the night with us? I really like her, and we want to watch more movies." It was only then she noticed Gray was with Alice. "You met Gray. Tooter is his dog ya know. Did you get a new dog, Gray? It looks hurt. What happened to it?"

Alice squatted to get on the little girl's level. "Maria, this dog is Warren, and she did get hurt, but some really good people saved her. Professor Jorgen has been taking care of her and helping her get better. He asked if you and I could help him out by letting her stay with us sometimes. Would you like that?"

Maria's eyes grew wide with excitement. "Oh, yes! Can she sleep in my bed?"

Alice was reluctant to agree despite knowing how happy it would make Maria. "Uh, well, we'll have to see about that. We don't even know if she likes sleeping in beds. Plus, she's still healing and probably sore. Sleeping with a wiggly munchkin might not be the best idea for her right now."

Maria was clearly heartbroken. "I won't wiggle. I promise."

Seeing the disappointment on the child's face, Alice decided to make her an offer. "Tell ya what, if it is okay with Gray, Grace can spend the night, and you two can watch movies. When it's bedtime, we'll make Warren a bed of her own on the floor right next to your bed. Deal?"

Hearing that perked Maria up. "Deal! Gray, can we? Please!"

Gray tapped her nose with his finger. "When you ask so sweet, how could I say no? Where is Grace anyway?"

"She's coming. Some of the other kids wanted to pet Tooter before we left. I'll go get her. Be right back!"

Watching Maria skip away, Alice smiled. "You just made a little girl very happy. I don't know what it is about Grace, but she is obviously special to Maria. Maria has never really associated much with any of the other kids, much less wanted one of them to sleep over. You and your friends have a knack for finding special kids."

"Well, Capp kind of made this one."

"Join us. We'll make popcorn and enjoy

Halloweentown with the girls. If you're a really good boy, we might even watch Hocus Pocus."

"That's the best offer I've had in a long time."

Capp rubbed his eyes, trying to shake the cobwebs from his mind, as he made his way to the ground floor of the hospital where he found Jordan sitting at the nurses' station in the emergency room. His notebook was in front of him. From what Capp could see, Jordan had written quite a bit in it during the night.

"Morning," Capp yawned.

"Morning. How did you sleep?"

"Like a log apparently. Why didn't you wake me up for my shift to stand watch?"

"I knew I wouldn't be able to sleep, had too many ideas rolling around in my head. Anyway, you have a big morning ahead of you and needed to be well-rested for it."

"What big morning? I did want to walk the town with you and go over some of those plans of yours. They're excellent plans. Thought we could visualize them better if we inspect the town. Other than that, my morning is wide open."

"You mean the plans are good for a kid."

"Uh, no. If that was what I meant, that's what I would have said. Those plans of yours are excellent. Excellent plans drawn up by an intelligent young man. Now, what did you mean about this morning, and where is Doctor Popal? I went to check on him when I woke up, but he wasn't in his room or the nursery."

"Doc is making us breakfast. Said today was a special

day and wanted to make us a special breakfast. I believe he mentioned coffee, omelets, hashbrowns, bacon, and biscuits."

"Mmm, you had me at coffee."

"And this morning is big because you're going back to Sandbox to help the others convince everyone what we're doing, what we're planning, and the melds are all good things. You're going to help them see this is how we save humanity."

"I'm not leaving you here alone. That wasn't the plan."

"I won't be alone. I radioed Chester and asked him to come take your place. He'll be here shortly."

"Why?"

"Capp the last two people anybody will take seriously are me and Chester, and don't argue with me on it, we both know it's true. They see me as a naïve kid and Chester as a screwup. You, Hobo, JC, and Gray don't see us that way, but the others do. I understand why they do though. We will eventually prove them wrong, but today they will only see a kid and a screwup. We would be of no help at that meeting, but they look at you and the others very differently. They see you as strong, capable, and intelligent; as a leader. That's who those people need to hear from today."

Capp wanted to argue with him. He wanted to be able to honestly tell him it wasn't true, but he couldn't. He'd heard the whispers about Chester and his drinking problem, and he knew because of Jordan's young age and childlike mannerisms they did view him as a kid. He desperately wished they could hear all the wisdom and maturity coming from Jordan in that moment. He knew if they heard it, they'd never think of him as a kid again. "You're right, especially the part about proving them wrong one day."

"For today, you make them see how important what we're doing is. Make them see Sandbox must be more than just walls to survive behind. It has to be what JC and Mike originally created it to be, a place to learn, to grow, and to nurture creativity. It has to be a place to dream and reach for the stars. If we don't have a place for that then there's no point in living. I know I don't want to live without those. As afraid of the melds as they may be, they have to see the melds are not only still partially us, but they're also the hope so many need and the best chance we have of making the whole world a safer place to dream. You have to make them see that."

"I'll do the best I can, promise."

"This is going to be hard for a lot of them to swallow. You'll have to do better than your best."

Suddenly they heard rattling coming down the hall toward them. Jordan jumped from his seat, and they both drew their weapons. The sound grew louder as it got closer. They were relieved when they saw Doctor Popal round the corner pushing a cart loaded with food.

Popal froze when he saw them. "I know I'm not the best cook in the world, but my food is not bad enough to evoke violence."

Capp, Gray, Hobo, and Professor Jorgen sat at the table in the meeting room while JC paced. All of them were nervous and feeling the pressure of what they were about to do. Each of them was acutely aware of the fact that what they were about to do had all the potential in the world to go wrong, but they knew JC, as their leader and founder of Sandbox, had more pressure on him than anyone.

"Okay," JC began, stopping to look out the window, "run through the plan once more."

"I'll speak first," Hobo said. "I'll tell them the story starting from Russo up until just before the discovery of Doctor Popal. At that point, I'll bring Gray out."

Gray quickly recited his role in the plan. "I'll tell everyone about Doctor Popal, Doctor Monroe, and Timothy, putting emphasis on how Doctor Monroe cares for Timothy and how human she acts. After I am done I'll call Professor Jorgen up."

Professor Jorgen shifted nervously in his chair. "I will explain the scientific implications of Mike, Doctor Monroe, and Timothy. I will tell them of the progress I've seen in Mike and the testing we plan to conduct. Then I will bring Mike out to show them how he is different from the afflicted before giving the floor to Capp."

Capp nodded to Jorgen. "I will then discuss our plans for Sandbox, the town, the bunker, and the hospital. I'll let them know how we plan to keep them safe, including that while we want to keep the melds alive, if they ever become a threat, we will not hesitate to put them down."

"Melds," Gray asked.

"Jordan started calling them that. I guess I picked it up."

JC turned back to them. "Melds you say? I like it. We

need a way to differentiate them from the afflicted."

"Does everyone like the term," Gray asked, to which everyone responded in the affirmative. "Good. Maybe we should do something to encourage everyone to use it. Maybe pass some sort of ordinance."

JC took a seat at the table. "As much as I like the sound of that, I don't' think it's a good idea. If people feel they're being forced, they could very likely become more resentful of the melds and us right along with them."

"Better to just use the term as much as possible, and if someone calls them afflicted, we politely correct them," Hobo offered.

JC pointed at Hobo. "That's the best course of action for the time being."

"That's settled then," Jorgen said. "Totally off topic, but could someone remind me why JC isn't speaking to them?"

JC sighed. "Professor, I've already covered that. I'm not speaking because I'm not what most would consider a people person. Sometimes when I say things they aren't taken as I intend them. Is it my tone? Is it my facial expressions? I don't know. What I do know is today is much too important for whatever it is to cause miscommunication."

"It's everything about you, you monster."

Exasperated, JC threw his head back. "Not now, GLaDIS!"

Clara poked her head in the room. "You boys ready? It's showtime."

Hobo stood, pulled a package from inside his coat, and walked around the table placing a cookie in front of each person. "I figured Hobo Cookies were in order. You know, a little something for the nerves."

Gray picked up his cookie. "Anybody got milk?"

Chester flipped through Jordan's notebook. "Capp's right, you have some really good plans here. These will help make everything more secure and run more smoothly."

"That's my hope," Jordan answered from the ER doorway where he was taking measurements. "Think they've started yet?"

Chester looked at his watch. "Should have. Remember, it will take a while. Be patient."

"What if it goes wrong though? What if they all decide to turn on JC and the others? They could hurt Mike or come here to put down Lauren and Timothy. We have to be prepared to defend them if that happens. Are you ready to do that if it comes to it? I mean, if the melds were a threat it would be different, but right now, they're still innocent."

"I'll do whatever is necessary to defend them and back you."

"To be on the safe side, let's make sure all the other hospital doors are locked. I want this to be the only point we have to defend if things go south."

"Let me get this straight," a man in the crowd shouted. "First you want us to believe these things, these afflicted, have some sort of feelings. Then you want us to believe they're harmless, and on top of all of that, you want us to be okay with you bringing one of them in here and hiding it from all of us. Does that about sum it up?"

Jorgen was flustered. He hadn't even gotten to bring Mike out because the people were continuously shouting or hurling questions at him. "Heath, as I have asked multiple times, please, save questions until I am through. At that time I will be glad to answer any and all questions to the best of my knowledge."

"They're shredding him," Gray whispered to no one particular.

Alice heard him. "They didn't make it very easy for you or Hobo either."

"No, they didn't," Capp agreed, "but they are really tearing into the professor. Hobo, that Heath guy seems to have tried to stir the pot since the minute you first started speaking. What do you now about him?"

"Let's see, he came here about a month ago with his two brothers and a small group. He and his brothers are very much the outdoorsy, rough, good, old boy types if you know what I mean. They were hateful and snarky, but Heath more so than the others. They very much remind me of the town bully and his henchmen. We were nervous about taking them in, but they were good shots and good hunters. Besides, we couldn't bring ourselves to leave anyone out there to die."

Capp watched Jorgen struggling to get a word in as Heath continued to rile the crowd. "You guys have Mike ready. I'll let you know when to bring him out." With that, he walked over to stand next to Jorgen. "Excuse me, folks," he said in a slightly raised voice. When the crowd didn't respond he decided he needed to get louder. “Excuse me, folks,” he shouted, a heavy firmness in his tone. The crowd quieted down considerably. “Thank you, I appreciate that. Folks, we understand the shock and possibly fear you must be feeling. We understand your anger too. Don’t you think we went through all the same emotions? I can tell you truthfully that we did. You wouldn’t be human if you didn’t feel all those things. The things you’ve been told today are not things we’ve ever encountered in the past, but then again, neither are the afflicted. The long and short of it is the world we live in is not the same world we grew up in. This is a totally new world full of things we’ve never encountered, and while some of them are bad things, not all of them have to be. We don’t believe the melds are.”

“What are melds,” asked Trina.

Jorgen stepped forward. “They are a mix of human and something else. Could that something else be afflicted? Possibly. I won’t lie to any of you, some of the characteristics they display are similar to those shown by the afflicted, however, they also display characteristics that are very much human.”

“Let us show you.” Capp motioned for Mike to be brought out.

“Okay, big guy, it’s time,” Gray softly told Mike. He looked at the handcuffs and chain they’d bound Mike with. A pang of guilt washed over him. “I am so sorry about those, but we have to make sure everybody feels safe. I still don’t like it though.”

Mike grasped Gray’s hand and gave it a tender squeeze. The look in his eyes told Gray he understood and conveyed the fear he felt without a word being uttered.

Gray led Mike out while Hobo led an afflicted out. The crowd collectively gasped, and many of them took several steps back. Mike watched them calmly while the afflicted jerked and snarled. Some of those who had known Mike had a hard time looking at him, and some shed tears.

Heath sneered. “Looks like two corpses to me. You say these melds have some things in common with the afflicted. Would one of those things be eating humans? Just where are y’all getting their food?”

Professor Jorgen decided to field that question. “Frankly, we are unsure if they crave human flesh. We have only encountered the three melds I told you about, including Mike here. To our knowledge, none of them have consumed human flesh. I can tell you for certain that Mike has not, and he has displayed no aggression toward the living people. The melds have been surviving on raw animal meat, but we have been experimenting with other foods. Mike drank coffee and eaten deli meats. Doctor Popal’s infant meld, Timothy, has been taking pureed animal meat with baby formula from a bottle. We have never given them human flesh, and we will not give them human flesh.”

Heath pulled his pistol, first leveling it at the afflicted then at Mike. “I hear you saying a lot, but what I’m not hearing you say is you can guarantee us they won’t decide to take a chunk out of one of us one day.”

Watching from a few feet away, JC felt his heart in his throat. He was witnessing the possible destruction of his beloved cousin and also humanity’s best hope. He fought the urge to rush Heath, opting to slip away unnoticed.

Capp and Gray placed themselves in front of Mike.

"Hold on there, Heath," Capp demanded. "The truth is that as it stands, we can't promise you such a thing. We've told you everything we know so far. It will take time to learn more, but I can promise you during that time they will be contained and monitored every hour of every day. We are in no way prepared to just turn them loose to walk among you. I'll also promise if they ever become a threat they will be put down. I'll do it myself if it comes to that."

Heath waved his gun in the direction of the afflicted Hobo had. "What about that one? Have y'all been keeping it here without telling us too? Is that one of your melds?"

Capp shook his head emphatically. "No, it's nothing like that! It's a random afflicted we captured this morning. We only brought it in to show all of you the difference between it and Mike." He pointed to the afflicted, which had increased its snarling and jerking movements. "Look at how it's acting. It is aggressive with no feelings or thought process behind that aggression. Mike, on the other hand, is calm, and as you can see, he is alert and fully aware of his surroundings."

Alice could see Capp was getting through to some of them, but a considerable amount of them were still on the fence or worse, leaning more toward Heath's train of thought. She knew they had to sway most, if not all, to their side, otherwise everything could fall apart at an alarming rate. She dashed over to Hobo and addressed the anxious crowd. "Everybody, please, listen to me for just a moment. I believe all of you know I was out on the road among the afflicted before I was brought here, and since then I've tried to continue the work of the person who rescued me by going in search of other survivors. Some of you are people I found during some of those excursions. I know all too well what the afflicted are capable of and the fear they evoke in us, and I see a distinct difference between them and the melds. I feel that awful fear of the afflicted, but I also feel the hope the melds offer us. For those of you I brought to Sandbox, surely you must know I would never advocate for anything that jeopardized your lives. That would essentially render everything I've done pointless. More than that, it would render everything done by the person who saved me pointless, and I would never do that to her." She looked at the afflicted. "I'll prove to you the melds are different from the afflicted."

Heath didn't lower his gun, but he watched on in anticipation with everyone else as Alice rolled up her sleeve and stepped closer to the afflicted. Hobo tightened his grip on the chain around the afflicted's neck. "Alice, what are you doing? This was not part of the plan."

"Just trust me, and for God's sake, don't let that thing bite me."

Alice slowly raised her arm to within mere inches of the afflicted's mouth, exposing her wrist to it. The afflicted pulled harder against the chain with a strength that shocked Hobo. It snapped at Alice with such force the sound of its teeth connecting with each other could be heard by everyone. Alice winced with each snap of those teeth, but she didn't budge.

Mike began to grunt and tried to jerk free from Gray. "No," he half growled.

Hearing him say that one word shocked the crowd, including Heath who lowered his gun slightly. "What the hell?"

JC had worked his way around to put himself in position just a couple of feet behind Heath. When Heath lowered his gun, JC took the opportunity to strike. He rushed forward with his fist raised and brought it down in the bend of Heath's elbow causing him to drop the gun. Before Heath could react, JC kicked him in the back of his knee. Heath dropped to the ground as the rest of the crowd scrambled to get away from them. JC swiftly retrieved Heath's gun and jabbed its barrel firmly against Heath's chest.

"You'd better learn how to act civilly in a community such as this," JC hissed. "Your actions here today have been reckless at best. You put people in danger. I've heard about the way you've been acting since you came to Sandbox. You like to impose your will on others and frighten them. You now have three options to pick from. Number one, you change your behavior and become a kind and productive member of this village. Number two, if you are not willing to do number one, you pack your crap and leave. Number three, if you are not willing to do either of the first two options, I will put a bullet through your heart right now and send you to walk with the afflicted. The choice is yours."

Heath glared at JC. "Fine, I'll be cool." He looked at the gun barrel still against his chest. His face and tone softened. "Look, I overreacted. I was freaked out. I'm sorry. I'll do better."

JC hesitated before removing the gun from Heath's chest and helping him up. He turned to walk away when Heath asked for his gun. JC never turned to look at him.

"I think you can do without it for a while. You'll get it back later, maybe."

Alice again addressed the crowd. "Guys, please, allow me to make the point of my demonstration." She paused while everyone settled back down. "Okay, great. You all saw how this afflicted reacted to me and how Mike reacted."

"Yeah, looked like they both wanted to eat you," someone shouted.

"No, not at all. Mike not only spoke, but he was trying to warn me. Alright, let's say his intentions weren't clear enough. Let's see what he does now. Gray, give Mike some slack, please." Gray did as she instructed, and she walked right up to Mike. "Hey, you okay, Mike? A lot of excitement and commotion, huh? Well, I want you to know it's all okay. We're all good here, but I was hoping you could help me explain Warren to them. Not the dog but the lady."

Mike grinned sheepishly and used his hands to trace the silhouette of a woman's curves just as he had the night before. "Roberta."

"That's new," Hobo muttered to himself. "Haven't seen him do that before."

Clara and Bobby, who'd been confused as to who Roberta Warren was the night before, snickered because JC had explained it to them after their poker game, even showing them a picture of Warren.

"Mike's not wrong," Bobby whispered to Clara.

Clara smiled up at her husband. "I'm woman enough to admit it's true."

"What's he doing, and who is Roberta," Paytan asked.

Capp, just as confused as most everyone else, shrugged.

"I'm not sure. This is new for me. Alice, care to explain?"

"Certainly. How many of you watched Z Nation?" Several raised their hands. "Excellent! Then you will know who Roberta Warren is."

Upon hearing that, those who had raised their hands smiled and nodded. Some even imitated Mike's silhouette tracing. It was obvious they got it.

"Alice, dear," Clara called. "You should explain for those who never watched the show."

"Oh, yeah, of course. *Z Nation* was a show about a zombie apocalypse. It featured a character named Roberta Warren. She was badass and gorgeous." She traced the silhouette.

"I can't believe I didn't pick up on that," Capp exclaimed. "I love *Z Nation*!"

Alice offered a hand to Mike, and he took it. Hand in hand they took a few steps closer to the crowd. "Mike loved Z Nation too," Alice informed them. "As close as I was to him, he didn't try to bite me. Instead, he recalled his love for the show and the beauty of one of its leading women. Now he stands here holding my hand calmly, no signs of aggression at all. Do you see the difference between the melds and the afflicted now?"

Capp expanded on Alice's question. "Do you see the humanity in the melds now? Will you allow me to share with you the plans we have for the melds, the town, the hospital, the bunker, Sandbox, and for keeping you safe? Will you hear me out? I have so much to share with you, and my hope is when I finish, you'll see, as a very smart man recently told me, Sandbox has to be a place for more than just surviving. It must be a place to dream and reach for the stars."

Jordan sat on a bench right outside the emergency room doors. The radio lay next to him. He was trying to forget it was there while simultaneously wishing anyone's voice from Sandbox would come across it.

"There you are," Doctor Popal exclaimed as he and Chester walked out of the hospital. "Any word yet?"

Jordan looked at the radio. "Not yet. I'm starting to wonder if that thing is broken."

They heard the distinct sound of an approaching vehicle. Jordan sprang from the bench and pushed Doctor Popal back into the building.

"Think it's friend or foe," Jordan asked as he positioned himself behind a pillar opposite Chester.

"Could be either, but I'm leaning toward foe or at least a stranger because the friends were supposed to contact us. Weren't they?"

A truck pulled into the parking lot followed by a car and a bus. Jordan squinted, straining to see who was in the vehicles, but the sun's glare obstructed his view. He could make out the shape of someone getting out of the truck and walking toward the hospital. He was relieved when he heard Capp's voice.

"Hey, Gray," Capp called, "get everybody organized right here while I find Jordan and Chester."

Jordan stepped from behind the pillar. "You won't have to go far to find us."

Capp jumped. “Jesus! You scared the hell out of me!”

Jordan looked over Capp’s shoulder at the vehicles. “Sorry about that. Who all is out there? How did it go?”

“It was touch and go, but for the most part, everybody’s on board.”

Jordan breathed a sigh of relief. “You did it! You pulled it off.”

“No, we all did, including you. Some of the words that seemed to reach them the most were words I borrowed from you.”

“Why didn’t you radio us to let us know?”

Capp put an arm around Jordan’s shoulders, walking him in the direction of the vehicles, and motioning for Chester and Popal to follow. “I wanted to give you the good news in person, and all of these good folks had reasons for coming too. They wanted to see the town, meet Doctor Popal, see Doctor Monroe and Timothy, and they wanted to hear some of your plans and find out how they can help you with them.”

Although Jordan didn’t vocally respond, Capp saw a smile spread across his face and the pride welling inside him.

Jordan saw Gray standing next to the bus as people were getting off it and waved to him. Gray waved back, but then Jordan froze. He blinked hard and rubbed his eyes. He was positive he was seeing things.

Capp took notice of the shift in Jordan’s demeanor. “Hey, you okay?” His eyes followed Jordan’s gaze to someone getting off the bus. “Do you know her?”

“It can’t be,” Jordan mumbled in disbelief.

Alice stepped off the bus and looked to see who Gray was waving at. Her eyes widened, and she started to shake when she saw Jordan. “Oh, my God. Oh, my God! Is this real?” She clutched Gray’s arm. “This isn’t a dream, is it?”

“Mama,” Jordan cried out.

Alice started running to him. Jordan, still frozen watched her. He held his breath, scared she would disappear. She was nearly to him when he saw something flash on the hillside behind Danterford’s. He was horrified to realize it was a laser sight, and it was aimed at Chester’s stomach. He shoved Chester to the ground, out of the line of fire, just as the arrow intended for Chester tore through his flesh.

“Everybody, get inside now,” Capp yelled.

Alice screamed. “No! No, no, no!”

Gray caught up to Alice and pulled her down, shielding her with his own body. She tried to push him away, desperately attempting to claw her way to her son.

Chester grabbed one shoulder of Jordan’s shirt, and Capp grabbed the other. Together they dragged him into the emergency room entrance where Doctor Popal had a stretcher waiting.

“Lay him up here,” Popal ordered.

Gray held Alice’s face in his hands. “Look at me, Alice. Look at me! We’re going to get to him.” He cautiously rose to a crouched position. He scanned the hillside for any signs of movement or the laser sight. When he saw nothing, he decided it was time to move. He stood and pulled Alice up. “Go, go, go!”

She did as he instructed. She reached the hospital doors only a few steps ahead of him, but neither of them slowed down until they reached Jordan. They watched Doctor Popal examine Jordan's wound, the arrow still protruding from just below his sternum. Jordan was moaning and gasping for air. Gray asked Popal if the arrow had punctured a lung.

"No. It doesn't appear it hit any of his organs or major arteries, yet, his breathing is labored, and his lips are turning blue. It makes no sense."

Capp passed Gray a piece of paper. "This was on the arrow."

Gray read the message scribbled on the paper aloud. "You shouldn't have interfered. Now we're watching." He crumbled the paper into a ball. "It has to be the asylum."

Alice held Jordan's hand and stroked his head. "Baby, I'm here."

"Mama, I'm so sorry," he managed to get out between gasps.

"No, baby! You stop that. I'm the one who should apologize. I wanted to be a good parent so badly, but I made so many mistakes. I am sorry, my sweet boy. I always loved you, Chris, and Amber though. Please, don't ever doubt that."

"I love you, Mama. I came to Virginia to look for you."

"I'm right here, baby, and I will never leave you again."

Chester, standing on the other side of the stretcher, placed a hand on Jordan's shoulder. "I'll never be able to properly repay you for everything you've done for me, but I promise I'm going to spend the rest of my life trying."

"We're even now, Chester." Jordan turned his head

to look at Capp standing next to Chester. "Don't let them to forget they have to reach for the stars."

"You'll make sure they don't forget," Capp insisted.

Jordan turned his attention to Gray. "You've been there for me since that first day you found us in Arizona, but I need you to do two more things for me."

"Anything, just tell me what you need."

Jordan's gasping was increasing, but he was determined to say what he had on his mind. "Make sure Mama gets to Chris and Amber, that's important. The other thing is if I turn afflicted instead of meld, you deal with it. Don't let Mama do it."

Alice, crying hysterically, gripped his hand tighter. "Don't you say that! You're going to be fine. Sure, it'll take you time to heal, but once you have, we'll all go to Chris and Amber. Now that I know they're alive too we'll all be together again. You're going to be fine."

Jordan mustered his strength to squeeze her hand. "I love you, Mama. Tell Chris and Amber I love them too, and Gray, I love you too, Dad."

Suddenly his eyes rolled back, he began to seize, and foam bubbled from his lips. It stopped just as suddenly as it had started, and Jordan's body went limp. Popal checked for a pulse then listened for a heartbeat.

"Capp, I assume the military taught you how to use one of these," Popal said as he retrieved a bag valve mask and tossed it to Capp.

"Sure did."

"Good. Bag him. I'll do compressions."

Gray, Alice, and the others watched as Popal and Capp

worked to save Jordan. Many of them were audibly sobbing, others were silently praying.

JC placed his radio on the kitchen counter, Chester had radioed with an update on the events at the hospital and Jordan's condition, leaving JC and Hobo dumbfounded.

"I...I...," Hobo stuttered. "I can't believe it. He and Alice were looking for each other all this time, and now they may lose each other all over again. It can't go this way."

They didn't have time to collect themselves from the shock before Clara burst through the door. "JC, you'd better get to the communications room. We were testing the new CB and antenna, and we got a response from someone. He asked for you by name."

"That's strange. Did he tell you who he was," JC asked.

"He said he was Russo."

Popal wiped the sweat from his brow as he climbed down off the stretcher. "Capp, you can stop. There's nothing more we can do for him."

Alice released a gut-wrenching, mournful scream.

Gray moved closer to the side of the stretcher. "There's something I can do for him." Within seconds Jordan's body began to twitch. Soon after his eyes opened, he sat up, snarled, and lunged at Alice. Gray swiftly drove his knife into Jordan's ear and twisted. Jordan's body went limp once again, and Gray gently laid him back on the stretcher. "I love you too, son."

Gray sprinted to the parking lot. He drew his gun and fired random shots at the hillside the arrow had come from. He continued to fire until he was out of ammo. "I hope you are watching because I want my face to be the last thing you all see when I kill you! Tell Norris I am coming to kill every last one of you! You hear me," he yelled. "I'm going to gut all of you bastards!"

SANDBOX SURVIVORS

J.C.'s Channel- JC should consider a career in writing. His love of the game combined with his ability to create and voice his own storylines has made him a favorite among viewers. Watching JC is like watching a good television show. Add his great personality to the mix, and he has a lot of people DOOOOOOMED to binge watch. Mike, pass the popcorn.

YouTube: @JCsChannel
Twitch: https://www.twitch.tv/jc_lc
Twitter: @JC_Channel

Capp00- Capp's even, mild mannered tone is in stark contrast to his adventurous nature in-game. His willingness to try anything for the sake of the game has made him a hit with viewers. With his trusty sidekick, Sylvia, Capp will try any stunt that he and even viewers can think up. His tests are always entertaining and educational. Sylvia tested, Capp approved.

Youtube: @capp00
Twitch: https://www.twitch.tv/capp00
Twitter: @Capp00

GrayGhostZoro- Gray may be new to the world of making videos and streaming, but he's a veteran when it comes to gaming. He's always had a love for the game in all its many forms, and now he uses it to get to know more people in the gaming community on a personal level. Friendly and a little goofy at times, this southern goofball is one to watch. Hauntingly entertaining.

YouTube: @GrayGhostZoro

Twitch: www.twitch.tv/grayghost_zoro
Twitter: @GrayGhost_Zoro

TheHoboJesus- Hobo is truly one of the most kind-hearted members of the gaming community you will ever find. While he is very blunt and to the point, he is also sweet and fun-loving. He is someone who has never met a stranger and has a love of both people and animals much like that of his mother who ran a cat rescue for much of her life. Oh, and in case you were wondering, Hobo Cookies are a thing!

Twitch: www.twitch.tv/thehobojesus
Twitter: @The_Hobo_Jesus

About the Author

Mandy was born in middle Tennessee along the Alabama border, an area rich in history & storytelling. From the time she could talk, Mandy loved nothing more than telling stories which naturally progressed into her love of writing. At a young age she was lucky enough to have the privilege of meeting the late, great author, Gregory Mcdonald whose inspiration & influence she carries with her to this day.

Mandy is a proud mother & grandmother. She resides in Virginia with her husband, Michael, & their family of fur babies.

There's more to tell, but she'd much rather tell you herself. Listed below are a number of ways to hear it straight from the horse's mouth.

Bluesky: @mandycmoore.bsky.social

Instagram and Threads: @mandyc_moore

Website: cmstarscreations.com

YouTube: @CMStars_Creations

Discord and Other Links: linktr.ee/cmstarscreations

CM STARS CREATIONS SUPPORTERS & FRIENDS

While there have been so many who have supported me, Gray, and CM Stars Creations, and we appreciate them all, there have been some who have been there since the very beginning or gone above and beyond anything we could have hoped for. I just wanted to take a moment to acknowledge them and thank them. To those folks I say thank you from the bottom of my heart, and I can't wait to see what we do together in the future!

Love,
Mandy

Brandon Connors **Lori Miller**

SummerofKorn **Miss Jamie**

Blue Haines **Aultra**

MORE FROM CM STARS PUBLICATIONS

www.ingramcontent.com/pod-product-compliance
Lightning Source LLC
LaVergne TN
LVHW091042080826
845145LV00002B/596

* 9 7 8 1 9 6 9 4 6 8 0 2 5 *